Tom

STEPHEN L. BRYANT

TATE PUBLISHING & *Enterprises*

Published by Tate Publishing & Enterprises, LLC
127 E. Trade Center Terrace | Mustang, Oklahoma 73064 USA
1.888.361.9473 | www.tatepublishing.com

Tate Publishing is committed to excellence in the publishing industry. The company reflects the philosophy established by the founders, based on Psalm 68:11,
"The Lord gave the word and great was the company of those who published it."

Book design copyright © 2010 by Tate Publishing, LLC. All rights reserved.
Cover design by Chris Webb
Interior design by Stefanie Rooney

Published in the United States of America

ISBN: 978-1-61663-857-3
1. Fiction, Crime
2. Fiction, Christian, General
10.07.09

Dedication

I have no talent but that given to me by our heavenly Father. Any inspiration from start to finish can only be credited to God. Therefore, this book is dedicated to everyone out there who has yet to realize his or her full potential. Open your heart and mind to God, and he in turn will open the world of opportunity to you. Simple as that.

I must also give credit to my loving bride, Pam. Without her, neither this nor my previous books would have been published. Thank you, sweetheart, for your dedication, commitment, faith, and love.

The Last Days

||||||||||||||||||||||||||||||||||||||||||||||||||||||||||||||

The temperature would break ninety-five degrees in several hours, with stifling humidity hovering just above 90 percent. It would, of course, rain. Most likely an ambush thunderstorm of sort before the slow-as-molasses guard brought Tom his evening meal of starch and soggy vegetables.

Thomas Lavon Tabor could predict the weather better than most meteorologists on any given day. He didn't know how such a talent developed but assumed it must be like his other unusual senses that bordered on extraordinary. He could hear the tiniest sound, smell things like a trained bloodhound, and sense most times what anyone nearby actually felt from deep within their soul. Of course, no one knew about his unbelievable artistic ability because Tom never told a single person. He never did because Thomas Tabor could not speak.

Tom knew, or rather sensed, that the sun stood at high noon and the billowing thunderclouds were just beginning to develop in the west. He listened to the distant, faint rumble and realized that the men in the yard would get a good old-fashioned soaking in an hour or so. No one else at the state penitentiary heard the thunder or smelled the rain in the air, but Tom did. And he did so in the ten-by-ten windowless cell on death row within the belly of the massive brick prison.

Tom visually surveyed the concrete cage and mentally inventoried his meager possessions. One pair of flip-flops utilized during his weekly shower, a tattered towel, washcloth, Nike tennis shoes without laces, and the new gray Dickies work shirt and pants folded neatly at the edge of the stainless-steel bed. The work clothes would only be worn once and, Tom knew, for a very short period of time.

The other items that occupied his man-made cave were the large cardboard calendar with "Whitey's Shell Station" across the top in bold black print and pictures of 1960s muscle cars at the bottom of each page. Lastly, he peered up to the only shelf in his cell where the King James Bible rested, collecting dust. *Not much,* he thought, *for fifty-two years of livin'.*

Tina Brown had been allowed to visit six weeks ago when she brought Tom the Bible, a writing tablet, a box of Bic pens, and a bag of peppermint candy.

Tom did not eat the candy, although he really liked peppermint, nor did he write a single word upon the tablet with the large, green-lined paper. He didn't write because he had concluded that there was nothing to say. And he did not eat the candy because the bag of peppermints was a special gift from the woman he loved.

Tom did believe in God, if only vaguely, and still remembered the stories about Jesus from his childhood Sunday school class with Tina, the only happy memory he could now recall. But Tom also believed that God had written him off a long time ago. Therefore, reading the Bible could provide no other emotion but anger. For all he knew, God was as dead as he would be in a matter of days.

Tom did allow a rare moment of happiness to creep into his being as he recalled his childhood adventures with Tina Marie Brown. He loved her then, and he loved her now—a feeling only he knew and the only meaningful memory he would take to the grave. All other thoughts were too dark and sinister to embrace.

When Tina visited him, the humiliation had been severe. The still beautiful girl pleaded with him the whole hour they were together.

"Thomas," she said, "you remember when Dad taught us about God's forgiveness and the love Jesus gives to every living being?"

"He can't answer you, missy," the huge black guard named Amos, spoke softly. "Tom ain't said a word since he's been here. Tom just don't speak, missy."

Tina's soft brown eyes looked deep into Tom's cold and painful expression of helplessness.

"Did something happen to you, Thomas? Is there a reason you can't speak? Can you write it on the pad I brought you?"

The soon-to-be-executed convict just stared across the many-times-painted metal table as tears of near unbearable pain ran slowly down his cheeks and fell quietly upon his clutched and trembling hands.

"Oh, Tom, my sweet, sweet Tom, what has this world done to you?" Tina clasped his big hands between her tiny, slender fingers and whispered, "Dear God in heaven, please forgive this precious soul. Heal his pain, dear Lord, and bring him into your love."

"I'm real sorry, missy, but I gots to get Tom back to his cell now." Amos sounded truly remorseful to have to make such a sad proclamation. "Maybe you can come back again, uh, you know, before, uh, the date."

"Maybe," Tina responded softly as she continued to watch Tom with innocent love long past but not forgotten.

"Would you like me to come back, Thomas?" It sounded more like a plea than a question.

Tom lifted his head slowly as he wiped the tears away with cuffed hands and slowly melted her soul as he responded with a headshake in the negative.

Tina felt her heart ache with the darkness of his pain. The torture from that place none of us like to go. Tom slowly turned toward Amos and the door leading him back to the living hell of death row.

"Jesus loves you, Tom. I'll pray for you every day. Oh, please read the Bible I gave you." Tina was now sobbing uncontrollably as the big black man shook his head in agony and wiped his own tears, leading Tom through the heavy metal door.

"I love you, Thomas Tabor—I've always loved you," Tina whispered not knowing that Tom heard every word. Tom sat quietly upon the paper-thin mattress in his cell, fighting the urge to scream out like a wild, wounded animal.

I love you too, Tina, and always will, he cried from within his heart.

Late one evening, Amos shuffled down the green and white checkered tiles between the cells on death row. As he quietly approached the cell of Thomas Tabor, he purposefully backed off into the shadows of the place of no second chances and carefully studied the man who looked inside you.

"Well, I'll be hung out dry," Amos whispered in astonishment as he watched Tom sitting quietly upon his bunk with the Bible resting beside him. To the best of his knowledge, the Bible had not moved from the shelf since Tina Brown had visited several weeks before.

He could see by the dim light that Tom had placed an X through the first four days of the month of August on the old car calendar. The prisoner had also drawn a large, dark circle around the date August 31, the day he'd be no more.

Tom suddenly looked up and locked eyes with the guard. Amos felt embarrassed for some strange reason, like he'd invaded Tom's most private zone. The two stared at each other for what seemed like an eternity to Amos, and then Tom smiled with warmth that filled the big man's heart.

Amos returned the smile, tipped his guard hat, and slowly moved back down the aisle on death row. He considered Tom special, a good man, and the soon-to-retire prison guard did not wish to see this poor soul executed.

Tom continued to watch the shadows where the guard had stood just seconds ago. The big black man's aura of kindness continued to radiate light that only Thomas Tabor, death row inmate, could see.

Tom smiled softly; reached down, gently stroking the holy Word of God; and picked up the writing tablet.

"My precious Tina Marie," he began to write.

The Beginning: Ironton, Ohio

The snow continued to fall at a ponderous pace, covering the gray and dismal existence of the dysfunctional family that lived in the three-room shack just north of Ironton, Ohio, bordered by Wayne National Forest.

With eight inches already on the ground, little Tom knew there would be no school this cold, forbidding morning, and he felt a moment of peace in knowing he would escape another day of humiliation.

He stiffly yet quietly moved from the big living room chair with the stuffing sneaking out from numerous holes in the red velvet fabric. The old chair, picked up from a neighbor's

STEPHEN L. BRYANT

yard before the garbage truck claimed ownership, served as the young boy's bed each night.

Tom covered his frail, shivering body with the patchwork quilt, clothed with nothing more than his dingy briefs and ragged tee shirt. He was so tired of his mother's greasy boyfriend, Big Earl, whipping him and his older, stupid brother Poke's taunting. No one knew better than he that his uncontrollable bed-wetting was not something he wished to do, yet it appeared to bring Big Earl and Poke great pleasure, as they called him "Pee Baby" or "Piss Boy."

Tom learned to focus his brain and would wake like clockwork each night at three a.m. This night would be no different as he tiptoed through the kitchen, his feet sticking to the filthy, freezing linoleum kitchen floor. Quietly opening the half-rotting back door, Tom pulled his dirty underwear down and peed a narrow stream into the cold air, watching the snow melt as he attempted to design a yellow seven, representing the age he would be tomorrow. There would be no cake, no presents, and most likely not even a happy-birthday hug from his mother, the town whore.

Tom shook from head to toe as he tugged his briefs up to his bony waist and pulled the heavy quilt tightly around his neck. At that moment, his scroungy mutt, Brown, appeared from below the house, looking nearly frozen to death.

"Come here, old dog," the boy whispered. "I won't let you die out here."

Tom knew he'd most likely get hollered at, or possibly get a medium-sized beating from Earl, but he didn't care. The boy's only real friend in the entire world was the flea-infested dog he named Brown, and if the truth be told, old Brown smelled a heck of a lot better than Big Earl.

Both boy and dog entered the house like ghosts on the bitter, savage night. It was almost as if the big, old canine sensed they were taking a major risk. Tom passed by the kitchen sink, glancing at the cracked and foggy mirror that hung from a rusty nail. He rubbed briskly against his nostrils, trying to wipe away the buildup of soot that clung to his nose like Etch A Sketch iron fillings.

The only heat in the shack came from the two portable kerosene heaters that filled the house with smoke and the occupants' lungs, hair, and noses with the pungent odor of burnt fuel. Tom was beginning to believe that he'd smell like kerosene for the rest of his life and hated the kids at school that called him "Oil Head."

The young boy did not return to the battered red velvet chair. He instead lit the oven, quietly opening the greasy stove's door, thus providing heat for the frigid kitchen. Tom believed his chances of escaping a beating on the morning of his seventh birthday were much improved by finishing the night near the back door, where he hoped to return the dog to the frozen landscape before first light. Plus, he knew that Big Earl would be grunting and farting like a pig before his mother awoke and started cursing her boyfriend.

Tom smiled, recalling the things he'd heard so many mornings coming from the tiny room next to the kitchen with the doorway covered by a stained, pink sheet for privacy.

"Holy cow, Earl!" his mother would bellow. "Get your lard ass out of bed and go to the outhouse. You smell like a pig, Earl Ray! What'd you do, crap your pants?"

Yeah, I'll be okay, Tom thought. Earl's farting would be better than a store-bought alarm clock. He could let Brown out, shut off the stove, and return to his red velvet perch before anyone knew the difference.

"Kiss my butt, Earl," Tom spoke softly and rested his arm on the old dog's massive neck.

Poke was the oldest of the idiots Tom's mother had given birth to. He stood six feet tall, was skinny, and was covered with festering pimples from his chest to his hairline. Now nearly seventeen, he was attempting to grow a shaggy goatee. Both his head and adolescent beard were the color of a too-old-to-eat carrot.

Poke quit school after he flunked the eighth grade for the third time and now worked at Miller's gas station for minimum wage. Big Earl and Poke were real tight. Mostly, Tom believed, it was because his older brother brought home a twelve-pack of Old Milwaukee each night. Greasy Earl and pimple-faced Poke would spend most evenings at the kitchen table chewing Red Man tobacco and guzzling warm beer while they looked at Doral in a disgusting, lewd fashion.

Tom's mother had four children, all by different fathers. The young boy believed his dad had been in The Marine Corps and lived outside the state. He had only seen him twice in the front yard, where it looked like he gave his mother a fistful of money each time, none of which he received.

Nobody knew who Poke's daddy was, but Tom knew for sure he was one ugly human being.

Doral, now pushing fifteen, knew her daddy, who lived in Huntington and owned Snow White Dry Cleaners. Her daddy sent money to Sherrell, the kid's mother, each and every month.

The last of the idiots was just simply called Baby, the only sibling Tom cared about. Four years old and severely retarded, Baby's dad was Big Earl, Sherrell's first cousin.

Poke stumbled into the kitchen at half past five that morning, rubbing his eyes with one grease-stained hand and scratching his private parts with the other.

"Holy crap!" Poke almost fell into the hot oven as he tripped over his little brother sprawled upon the kitchen floor.

"What the hell you doing in here, moron?" Poke hissed. "And what the hell is that half-breed mutt doing in this house?"

"He was freezing out there, Poke," Tom whispered.

"Well, get him out of the house now, you little asshole, or I'll tell Earl, and you'll get a serious butt whipping."

"But it's freezing outside, Poke! Please let Brown stay in the house till it's light."

"I don't give a rat's ass if the mutt freezes on the back steps!" Poke snarled, showing the green slime at the point between his teeth and gums. Poke grabbed at the large dog, and Brown snapped back with his powerful jaws.

"All right, you crazy mutt, that did it!" Poke reached behind the icebox, producing a Louisville Slugger baseball bat saved mostly for fights with the neighbors.

"Please, Poke, don't hurt Brown! I'll let him out."

Poke was a true-blue coward, and deep within, the dog scared the living crap out of him.

"Then do it, you little punk!" Saliva ran from the corner of Poke's mouth, glistening upon his scraggly orange beard.

"Come on, boy. I'm sorry." Tom wiped the tears from his eyes as he let the dog out the door and walked back to the living room, sobbing.

Poke stood at the back door as Brown growled in defiance toward the redheaded teenager, who attempted to pee on the dog.

Tom noticed Poke's Red Man tobacco pouch upon the coffee table and quickly opened it, straining to produce a little urine attack himself. This would not be the last time he peed in Poke's tobacco, an activity his goofy brother never seemed to notice.

The Friendship

|||||||||||||||||||||||||||||||||||||||||||||||||||||||||||||||||

Tom walked carefully upon the edge of the long dirt road that ran along small half-dead cedar trees intertwined with patches of briers that could entangle an elephant.

An early spring thaw had relegated the dirt path to black-ish purple slime, while soot-topped snow covered each side of the country lane leading to the paved highway a hundred yards away.

Tom chose not to walk through the purple mud and instead sunk ankle deep in the dirty snow along the side of the road.

The mushy, black snow oozed into his Salvation Army shoes from both the top and the large holes in the bottom of the soles. He wiggled his toes and mumbled obscenities, as he could already feel the moisture soaking into his dingy, white socks.

Tom hated where he lived, despised his mother and dysfunctional family, but nothing attacked his soul with more fear and loathing than catching the yellow school bus that would once again deliver him into the continuous hell of humiliation.

Tom noticed the yellow prison come to a halt as his inner self drifted toward the subconscious. He heard only the metallic sound of the sign, as it seemed to crawl out of the skin of the bus. "STOP," it read, as well as proclaimed as if a screeching voice from hell.

Yes, stop, Tom thought. *Please stop the hurt, the pain, the humiliation. Please stop the world and stop my life.* A very sad way for a seven-year-old child to face the day.

All the older kids ruled from the front seats of the yellow prison, which meant that Tom must run the gauntlet of humiliation twice a day throughout the school year. He grimaced and the tiny hairs on his arms stood at attention as he took the first two steps and heard the squishing sound from his wet, old shoes echo like a flash flood in a hidden forest hollow.

"Hey, Oil Head, got any fish in those boats on your feet?" the eighth grader bellowed.

Tom lowered his head and attempted to move toward the back of the bus, not seeing the fourth grader stick his foot out in the walkway.

The young boy tripped, flipping his tattered school books forward and falling on his brown paper lunch bag that contained one peanut butter and jelly sandwich he himself prepared that morning while his mother slept next to her cousin, Big Earl.

The bus roared with obscene laughter, and Tom wished with all his might that he were dead. Then the sweetest sound he had ever heard came out of nowhere, as if God decided to send an angel to his rescue.

"I picked up your books. Come back here and sit next to me."

Tom slowly got to his knees and looked into the eyes of the most beautiful person he could ever have dreamed of. Without saying a word, he followed the young girl to the last seat on the bus and quietly sat beside her.

"My name is Tina Marie Brown." Tom thought her voice sounded like the gentle wind sometimes did when it blew through the pines back by his secret hiding place.

"My name is Thomas Lavon Tabor," he almost whispered, not knowing why he'd given all three names. But he believed that if this angel spoke three names, it was only right to tell her all of his as well.

"I'm new here." The little girl smiled, and Tom thought she smelled like honeysuckle. "My daddy is gonna be the preacher at the New Bethel Methodist Church. Do you know where it's at?"

"Um, no. We don't go to church."

"Well then, we just have to invite you to my Sunday school class, seeing as you're my first new friend!"

Tom bit down hard on his lip to suppress the smile erupting in his heart.

My first new friend. His mind committed the statement to memory.

"What's Sunday school?" Tom asked with some hesitation.

"Well"—Tina beamed—"it's where you learn about Jesus and how to be a good person and love other people!"

"I think I'd like that," the young boy replied quietly, wondering if such a place could be real.

"Great!" Tina touched his pale arm. "I'll be your teacher about Jesus, Thomas Lavon Tabor!"

"Um, Tina." Tom fought for the words. "Do you ever walk through the woods?"

"Oh, yes!" She smiled with childish joy. "My daddy just bought us a house not a stone's throw from where the bus picked you up."

Tom now let the smile come out from ear to ear.

"Yeah? Well I know a place where every wildflower in the world grows. It's hidden and secret, but I'll show you if you'd like."

Tina wiggled in her seat with excitement, reaching out and squeezing Tom's hand.

Thomas Lavon Tabor had never felt so wonderful in all his life.

The Letter: August 4

||||||||||||||||||||||||||||||||||||||||||||||||||||||||||||||||||

My precious Tina Marie:

I am so sorry that I acted like a total imbecile when you visited me. As you now know, I lost my ability to speak in a tragic situation so many years ago.

Please believe me when I tell you that I felt complete and total humiliation when I walked into the prison visiting room to find the only person I had ever truly loved standing before me and couldn't even say hello.

I know you are happily married and have a wonderful family. So to see you there in this hellish prison was almost too much to bear.

Why would she come to see me? Why would she care? Just two of the many questions I asked myself after you had gone.

Then I knew the answer. I allowed my mind to go back in time, something I have refused to do for many a year. I recalled the first day I met you when we were both seven years old. You were, and still are, my only true friend.

For a man that has lived a half century, it is hard to admit that you have only loved one person during that time. Sadly for me, that's the way it is.

In twenty-seven days, I will be executed for the hideous crimes I committed. It is how it should be for a man who was worthless from beginning to end. I will walk to my death with but one regret; I know I disappointed you.

Your final act of kindness has touched an inner part of me that has lain dormant for so many years. I'd forgotten that such feelings could exist.

I have nothing to give anymore. No words of wisdom, righteous acts, or final contrition do I have to offer. And I only leave behind a solitary friend. Yes, I will go to my execution seeing the blue-eyed, blonde-haired angel that once said, "I picked up your books."

I do not believe God ever really loved me, Tina. Quite honestly, I do not believe that a God of love really exists. I don't say this to hurt you; I say it because I have lived in hell all my life.

That said, however, I would like to propose a deal to my only friend. In the next twenty-seven days, I will search the Bible you gave me. I will also write you the story of my life. In the end, we will see if I can find God, or we will see if after you have read my life story, you can believe that God ever knew me.

One thing is for sure, my precious Tina: one of us will change our mind. I will ask the guard, Amos, to deliver this letter and my story after my execution.

May your God be with you,
Tom

The Tabor Family

IIIIIIIIIIIIIIIIIIIIIIIIIIIIIIIIIIIIIIIIIIIIIIIIIIIIIIIIIIII

Sherrell Tabor entered the gates of purgatory as the youngest of eight children born to Harvey and Esther Davis, in a decimated coal-mining town east of the Kentucky and West Virginia border. Harvey and Esther were second cousins and became joined in marriage on Esther's fifteenth birthday. Harvey, then nineteen, had already worked in the coal mines for six years.

The entire lot of Tabor kids were semi-retarded and looked most times like photos from *LIFE Magazine* depicting Holocaust survivors. Sherrell, however, was different, which gave the coal-mining neighborhood reason to speculate that her daddy just might be somebody other than old, toothless Harvey.

At the age of thirteen, Sherrell was already developing into a beautiful, young woman. Nearly six feet tall and slender, she could have been an athlete, a model, or even a movie star if destiny had seen fit to place her anywhere except the coal miners' shack that tenuously clung to the West Virginia mountainside like a dying granddaddy-long-legs. Instead, her beauty and sensuality did not develop as an asset; rather they made her human bait for the illiterate band of walking-dead perverts that spewed forth from the mountainside like an evil virus.

Her older brother learned to sexually abuse Sherrell by following the example set by their father, who secretly knew that the young girl was not really his child and therefore, fair game.

Sherrell, on the other hand, knew that her mother and two older sisters watched her abuse openly and did nothing to stop it because they hated her beauty.

By the time Sherrell reached sixteen years of age, she had refined the art of male manipulation. Just about anything she wanted could be had rather easily. All Sherrell needed to do was catch some pervert looking her way, which guaranteed they would pay the price for her affections.

At seventeen, the young beauty gave birth to her first son. No one knew for sure who the father might be, but the only other person in the county with red hair was Mickey the moonshine runner, Sherrell's first cousin on her mother's side.

Mickey went to state prison for moon shining right before Sherrell's first son came into the world, and everyone thought it more than interesting that the girl somehow ended up with the distiller's black Lincoln.

The local menagerie of welfare hillbillies speculated often about where the name Poke came from, but everybody knew that Mickey's favorite meal at Sally's Diner was poke greens and hog jowl bacon.

"Guess the name was better than calling the boy hog jowls," some folks whispered.

After Poke's birth, Sherrell went to work for Paul Sheffield, who owned Snow White Cleaners. Paul was a wimpish fellow whose wife kept a tighter reign on him than most chained junkyard dogs.

Sherrell worked her way up to store manager, a feat not ignored by the wife of the owner. Before her nineteenth birthday, Sherrell became pregnant with her second child.

Soon after her tight belly began to expand, Mrs. Sheffield assumed the position of store manager at the Snow White Cleaners and Sherrell became unemployed.

The rumor mill in the small community began buzzing once again like mosquitoes at the outhouse light on an August night.

Sherrell quickly disappeared, although talk at Sally's Diner whispered that someone bought the girl a house somewhere in Ironton, Ohio.

Paul Sheffield carefully took three dollars a day from the Snow White Cleaners cash register without his domineering wife ever being the wiser. That money was placed in a plain white envelope and would appear like clockwork each month at the mailbox marked Nineteen Rural Route One, Ironton, Ohio.

Once a month, Sherrell would load up Poke and his baby sister, Doral, and drive home to her mother's house. She'd always give her momma a five-dollar bill from the plain white envelope before leaving for Huntington and the thrills waiting inside the Mountaineer Tavern. Sometimes Sherrell would be gone from her children overnight, and sometimes she wouldn't return for days, which would cost her an extra five.

The Mountaineer Tavern was the place to be at the end of the month in Huntington, West Virginia. Every coal miner with a dollar or two, and most of the farmers that sold a crop or a cow, came to the tavern at the month's end for a good old drunk and to participate in the cloggin' dance contest. Most of the patrons needed a bath, and some could have clearly used a good old-fashioned sheep dippin'.

Sherrell, of course, instantly became the main attraction. Every boy or man from sixteen to eighty fought to get in line for a dance with the West Virginia princess.

Josh Wildman sat quietly at the bar, sipping his draft beer and contemplating what officer's candidate school would be like when he reached the US Marine Corps training facility at Quantico, Virginia.

Sherrell hooped and hollered like a high school cheerleader after receiving a fifth of Old Grand Dad Whiskey, first-place prize for winning the cloggin' dance contest. Surrounded by men and boys of all ages, most of which smelled liked hay, coal, or worse, Sherrell caught her first glimpse of PFC Joshua Wildman sitting quietly all alone.

The young marine sat straight and silent in his crisp green uniform. Sherrell had never seen a man quite as handsome in her life. She moved quickly through the crowd of reeking wannabe lovers like honey rolling off a hot biscuit.

"Well, excuse me." She tried to sound confident, but her heart was doing cartwheels. "What do we have here? Could it be a real soldier boy?"

"No, ma'am." Josh's smile melted her every natural defense. "What you have here is a real United States Marine."

"Well, beg your pardon, I'm sure," she purred. "Buy a lonely young girl a drink, Mr. Marine?"

"It doesn't look like you're too lonely, miss, but I'd be honored to buy you a beer."

He's mine now. Sherrell secretly admired her God-given talent.

Josh Wildman left for OCS the next morning, and nine months later, Sherrell gave birth to Thomas Lavon Tabor, her third child.

At age thirty-one, the years of drinking, eating too much pork, and spending 50 percent of each day in bed left Sherrell Tabor looking like she might be in her midforties.

Living out in the middle of nowhere without transportation left the mother of three children few options. Then one day, out of the clear blue sky, Sherrell's middle brother appeared on the front steps with a case of beer and their cousin Big Earl, who made his living stealing anything from cars to chickens.

Sherrell's brother left after three days and eight cases of beer. But Big Earl Ray liked the way his cousin touched him, and he could steal stuff in Ironton, Ohio, he reckoned, as good as anywhere else.

Fifteen month's later, Sherrell gave birth to Baby. The child came into this world seriously handicapped and mentally deficient. Baby was never given a name and was ignored like an old, worn-out dog by the Tabor family. No one loved this pitiful little child except Tom, and he became her protector and caregiver.

The Browns

||||||||||||||||||||||||||||||||||||||||||||||||||||||||||||||||||

Brent Matthew Brown and his wife, Karen, met while attending a small Christian college in the northeast nearly thirteen years ago. Brent wanted to be a teacher and gave it his best shot for ten years after graduation. But hard as he tried, the teacher always felt like something important was missing in his life.

Karen completed her training as a registered nurse and found a good position at the VA Hospital in Louisville, Kentucky.

While Karen cared for the old and forgotten war veterans, she realized that the burden of dealing with such unloved souls took a heavy toll on her emotionally.

Brent settled in as the ninth grade math teacher at an inner-city high school that seemed to only produce children destined for a life of crime and poverty. Both Brent and Karen spent a great deal of time at the Broadway Church of the Nazarene, where Brent taught the adult Sunday school class. On Sundays, Brent and Karen tried desperately to forget the previous six days of the week.

Brent grew up in rural Indiana and spent most of his life enjoying the solitude of the fields and forest that surrounded his family's small farm. He longed for days gone by when as a child he would sit for hours and watch the snow geese land upon the lake. He could still recall, and most likely mimic the beautiful songs of at least a dozen wild birds. Brent remembered seeing, hearing, and even feeling God in those precious moments of peaceful reflection one can only find in nature's creation.

As teacher and registered nurse, the Browns lived a comfortable lifestyle, and being a frugal man, Brent had begun a savings and investment plan. Outside, they lived a perfect life. Inside, the tragedies of the VA Hospital and the hopelessness of the inner-city school were slowly destroying their very souls, and Brent knew they must escape.

As time passed, Karen became increasingly worried about their only child, Tina Marie, and what effect living in a big city might have on the young girl as she entered school.

After church one Sunday, Reverend Jesse Raborn asked Brent to take a ride with him. As they drove south through the country, their conversation ambled in simple chitchat. However, Brent could sense that something important would be said before the day ended.

As the old flathead Ford struggled to climb the winding steep roads toward the peak atop Mitchell Hill, Brent asked, "Just where are we headed, Brother Jesse?"

The good pastor, a strong, handsome man in his late sixties, turned his head to face his passenger and smiled broadly. "Well, Mr. Brent Brown, my brother, I'm going to take you to the place where I first found the Lord."

Brent looked quizzically at his pastor and did not say another word until the old Ford drove down a barely recognizable dirt road covered by knee-high weeds that might ensnare a healthy goat.

"Here we are!" Pastor Jesse bellowed. "Let's talk to God."

Without another word, the elderly pastor trampled through the waist-high thicket like a John Deere tractor in low gear. All Brent could do was follow and secretly wonder if his mentor had completely lost his mind.

"Ah, here we are, my boy!" The pastor pulled his starched handkerchief from his back pocket, wiping the sweat from his shining bald head. "God's rock, God's mountain, God's view!"

Brent could readily see that the spectacular view was well worth the trip. "It is indeed a beautiful spot, Pastor," he spoke in a reverent tone.

"Sit, boy—come here and sit next to me on this big, old rock God placed here thousands of years ago."

Brent did as the reverend commanded and instantly felt the Spirit of God surround them.

"Brent, my son, I have a story that I believe the Lord thinks you need hearin'."

The young schoolteacher could only look with uneasy expectation at the elderly pastor he loved so much.

"Now look way down there to the right between that big grove of oak trees. Can you see a pool of clean water that sits in the middle of the creek?"

"Yes, sir, I see it. The water seems to sparkle, doesn't it?"

"I guess it does, boy." The preacher laughed. "I guess it does, because there's been many a Christian baptized in that pool of water!"

"Is that where you were baptized, Brother Jesse?"

"Yes, sir, that's the place. Some fifty-six years ago. Back then it was different, son. Baptism Sundays were a thing to behold. The entire congregation dressed in white on both sides of the creek, singing *Amazing Grace*. I still remember the sun breaking through the branches of those big, old oak trees, dancing across the turquoise pool like fingers of God. It was alive, son! And when you came up out of that sweet, clear water, you knew the Holy Spirit was all over you."

The preacher became quiet for a long moment. "Now we have little plastic pools inside the church. People just want to be sprinkled so as not to get their fancy clothes wet. We've forgotten, Brent, where to find the Lord, I'm afraid."

Both men were purposefully quiet, as if allowing God to fill them up on this rock of ages overlooking the baptismal pool of natural beauty and serenity.

"After I was baptized, boy, the whole congregation went back to the church for dinner on the grounds. Well, even as a twelve-year-old, there was nothing more appealing or motivating for me than fried chicken, homemade tater salad, and apple pie. But after I came up out of that pool, I didn't want to eat, son. I wanted to talk to God!"

The preacher cocked his head in a funny way and looked up into the light blue sky as if seeing that moment now fifty-six years gone by.

"Yes, sir, boy, I disappeared into these woods and ran zig-zag up this hill like a billy goat that knew spring clover was in bloom at the top."

"That's a long, steep climb, Brother Jesse."

Jesse Raborn laughed in such a way that if you weren't nearby and watching him, you just might think you were hearing a twelve-year-old boy having one heck of a good time.

"Don't reckon I'd like to try it now, Brent, but back then" —He paused and smiled broadly—"I was running with God."

"So you made it to the top, and what happened?" Brent Brown could feel the story building.

"Well, I sat down here on this big, old rock, and a brief shower came down. You know, one of those warm summer rains that make you instantly feel clean and fresh."

"Yes, sir, I do know how that feels, and I miss it."

"Anywho, the shower lasted just a few seconds, and then the sun came back and it felt like its every ray was a shinin' on me. And then, Brent, God Almighty spoke to me. I know that sounds pretty farfetched, and I haven't told but just a handful of folk, but as sure as I live, boy, God talked to me that day."

"What did God say?" Brent inquired nervously.

"The Lord said, 'Jesse, my son, you are going to preach the Word of God.'"

"Amazing," was all Brent could mutter.

"Yes, it was and is. But that ain't the end, Brent. No, that ain't all the Lord's told me directly."

Brent just looked on in astonishment.

"I was walking out back of the church yesterday morning and knelt down at the prayer bench in the rose garden, as I do most mornings. Then I heard the voice of God again, riding upon the warm breeze that touched my face and replenished my soul."

After a moment of silence, Brent couldn't help himself. "And what did God say to you yesterday?"

"The Lord said that you, Brent Brown, are going to preach the Word of God."

Pastor Jesse Raborn was a well-respected elder in the Nazarene organization, and his word could be considered gospel within its hierarchy. When he heard that the small church in Ironton, Ohio, needed a pastor, Brent had no doubt God would be leading him to his destiny.

At first, Karen struggled with the idea. There was her job and their financial security to worry about. But after Brent's trip to the hillside with Brother Jesse, she knew the only choice rested in doing the will of God. Her husband would soon be delivering the gospel, and she would support that endeavor.

Pastor Brown and his lovely wife sat at the kitchen table inside their modest parsonage, discussing Brent's notes for his Sunday message, when they heard the squeaking brakes of the yellow school bus.

"Tina's home." Karen smiled like only a loving mother can.

Both parents watched as their beautiful seven-year-old raced up the long gravel driveway, laughing and jumping with joy as Lady, their golden retriever, met her with equal enthusiasm.

Tina leaped into her father's arms, shaking her long, silky, blonde hair in all directions while she laughed without a single burden or care in the world.

"How was school today?" her mother asked as she began to snap green beans into the strainer pot.

"Oh, Mommy!" she exclaimed, sucking in her breath with excitement. "I met the sweetest boy today. He's going to be my bestest friend!"

"Really now?" Her father smiled. "You're seven years old and already have a boyfriend?"

"Oh, don't be silly, Daddy!" Tina chirped. "He's not my boyfriend; he's my bestest friend."

"What's his name, honey?" Karen asked as she washed the beans in the kitchen sink.

"Thomas Lavon Tabor," she said. "He has three names, just like me!"

"Where's he live, baby?" Karen dried her hands on the checkerboard apron and pulled the little girl onto her lap.

"Over there, Mommy, in the woods." Tina climbed up on the wooden kitchen chair and pointed out the bay window above the sink.

Both parents leaned forward, squinting their eyes for focus as they sighted the dilapidated shack partially hidden by weeds and numerous trees. Karen gave a quick glance at her husband with more than skepticism.

"You can't tell a book by its cover, dear," he chided.

"You're right," Karen responded with sincere remorse in her voice.

"How old is your little friend?" Karen asked.

"Same as me, Mommy. He's so poor, Daddy, and I hate the way the other kids make fun of him."

"What do you mean, Tina?" Brent pulled a kitchen chair beside his wife and daughter.

"Well, his clothes are real poor, and he smells funny, and all the other boys make fun of him and pick fights because he's smaller than they are. You know, Daddy, I don't think Jesus likes those older boys."

Brent found himself lost for words, which happened often when his little girl proclaimed her own brand of wisdom.

"And guess what else, Daddy?"

"What, baby?"

"All Tom had in his lunch bag was a peanut butter and jelly sandwich. And it wasn't even wrapped in wax paper! I offered him some of my cookies and apple, but he just said no thank you. I think he was really hungry, Mommy, but just too proud to take 'em. I like him, Daddy. He's a really nice boy, just real poor I guess."

Karen wiped a tear away and whispered, "Unless you become as little children."

Brent smiled as he reached down and gently kissed his little girl. "The true meaning of being a Christian taught to us by a seven-year-old."

"Can Tom come over and play sometime, Daddy?"

"Sure he can, baby. Anytime he likes."

That Saturday morning, Reverend Brent Brown knocked softly upon the loose screen door, minus the top half of the screen. He was rather surprised when the huge, hairy man with the ample beer gut opened the back door and stood scratching his private parts.

"Whatever you got, we ain't buying!" the big man reeking of stale beer growled.

"Well, sir, I'm not selling anything but the love of God."

"Ask 'em if he's one of those Jehovah Witness freaks!" Poke bellowed from the kitchen table, also clothed in nothing more than his dingy underwear.

Earl ignored Poke and just stood there scratching himself like a flea-infested hound. "That's it?"

"Well, no, sir. You see, I'm the pastor at the Nazarene church just a half mile down the road. I wanted to invite you to Sunday services tomorrow."

Big Earl chuckled like he didn't believe this guy was really asking this gang of derelicts to go anywhere.

"Tell him we're usually hung over on Sunday mornings!" Poke laughed and lit a fresh Camel cigarette.

"Shut your mouth, Poke, you moron. Well thanks just the same, Preacher, but we got better things to do on Sunday." Earl laughed.

"I'd like to go." Brent knew it must be Tina's new friend.

"You don't go anywhere unless I tell ya, you little bastard!"

"Shut up, Earl Ray!" The almost attractive woman in a flimsy bathrobe pushed the smelly, big man out of her way.

"I'm sorry, Preacher, but as you can see, Big Earl and Poke ain't got no class. We're not churchgoing folks, but thanks just the same for asking."

"But I'd like to go, Mama," Tom pleaded.

Sherrell turned and looked at her youngest son, and for a moment, you could almost see love. She turned back to the preacher.

"Can the kid go by himself?"

"Yes, ma'am, he surely can. If you like, I'd be glad to pick him up at eight-thirty tomorrow."

"All right, then, he'll be cleaned and ready."

"Thank you, Mama," Tom whispered and kissed her hand.

"Um, miss, if it's okay, we'd be proud to have your son join us for dinner after church if you don't mind."

"Hell, Preacher, keep him long as you like for all I care!"

Brent just caught a glance at the dirty, little face with eyes that cried out, *Help me!*

STEPHEN L. BRYANT

The Letter: August 5

||||||||||||||||||||||||||||||||||||||||||||||||||||||||||||||||||||||||||||||||||

Amos just delivered my breakfast on the five-compartment metal tray. Runny scrambled eggs, two burnt sausage links I think, white bread, and some kind of orange drink that kinda tastes like weak Kool-Aid. Guess the warden don't want to execute a fat man, huh?

As I promised, Tina, I will attempt to tell you the story of my life and take a serious look at the Bible you so graciously provided.

I've decided that what little time I have left ain't going to be near enough to read the whole Bible, so it might be best just to open it and read whatever jumps out. And you know, Tina, that's what I did this morning, and guess what? I'm beginning to believe in God!

Allow me to explain that point. You see, I opened the Bible to the book of Job, and the old boy reminded me of myself. There's God—good, and there's Satan—evil. And then there is Job, stuck dead in the middle.

Yep, I guess I might be able to believe in God now. Of course, I must also have to accept Satan in the bargain. You know what else I believe now, Tina? The evil one just might have made a deal with God on me! Unfortunately, it looks mighty good that the old boy with horns and a tail is gonna win this bet!

So just how did Lucifer end up with my mind, body, and soul anyway? Let me begin by recalling one of the few beautiful days in my life ...

The Secret Place

||||||||||||||||||||||||||||||||||||||||||||||||||||||||||||||||||||||||

Tom thanked his mother profusely as she handed him the clean white shirt still warm from the ironing board. The boy tried to recall if his mom had ever ironed one of his shirts before.

"Do I look okay, Mom?" Tom inquired, needing reassurance.

Sherrell looked at her third child and wished she'd gone to the Dollar Store the night before and purchased the kid some new shoes and a pair of churchgoing pants. Instead, Sherrell opted to spend what little money she had dancing and drinking the night away with Big Earl, Poke, and their friends while Tom and Doral stayed home and watched Baby.

"You look just fine, son. As good as anybody else is gonna look at some hick church." Sherrell turned from the boy, hating the embarrassment she felt.

"Hey, Pee Boy!" Poke bellowed out as he belched in between words. "You'd better wipe that cow shit off your clod-hoppers before you stink up the whole church!"

Smack! The sound reverberated throughout the kitchen as Big Earl hit Poke hard behind his ears with an open hand.

"Get up off your skinny butt and clean the mud off your little brother's shoes, moron."

"Screw him, Earl," Poke moaned. "If he wants to be a Bible thumper, let him clean his own damn shoes."

"I said clean the boy's shoes, Poke, or I'll damn well clean 'em with your greasy face!"

Poke knew better than to argue with Big Earl, especially when the man had a king-sized hangover.

Poke got up and grabbed a dishtowel that wasn't much cleaner than Tom's shoes.

"Come here, you little punk," Poke muttered, low enough that only Tom heard him.

"Come over here, boy." Big Earl almost sounded kind, which surprised Tom. "If you gotta go to church, you best dress right."

Big Earl put the wide purple and green striped tie around the boy's collar, tying a double Windsor knot. "Now, tuck the long, skinny piece inside your shirt."

"There now, Sherrell." Earl smiled. "I think the boy looks good enough to go to Sunday meetin', don't you? Maybe the preacher can teach him to do his chores."

"Yeah, Earl, I guess he looks like my little preacher man!"

"Make me puke." Poke snarled and stormed out of the house.

Sherrell brushed Tom's hair one final time and held his face in her hands. "Now don't you do nothing to embarrass us today, Thomas Tabor."

"I won't, Mom. I promise."

Tom left through the front door to wait in the muddy yard for Reverend Brown to pick him up for Sunday school.

"Hey, Pee Boy!" Poke hissed from the side of the Tabor shack. "You look like a queer."

"Yeah?" Tom shot back. "Well, Poke, you are a queer!"

Tom laughed so hard it brought tears to his eyes as he skipped down the dirt road toward the highway to meet Mr. and Mrs. Brown and his new friend, Tina.

Karen Brown placed the big platter of smoldering fried chicken upon the oak table right in front of Tom, and he instantly panicked as his stomach growled loudly. This would be the first meal the boy ate since the lumpy oatmeal nearly twenty-four hours ago.

"Well, I'd say hurry up with the blessing, Reverend. I believe our guest of honor says it's time to eat." Karen leaned over and kissed Tom on the cheek, and he felt real love for the first time in his life.

Tom seemed hesitant to eat at first, but after watching Tina dig in like a lumberjack, he relaxed and ate until his belly felt like a ripe watermelon.

"Did you enjoy church today, Tom?" Brent inquired.

"Yes, sir, I really did. I never knew you could learn so much in one day."

"So what'd you learn, son?" Karen smiled, and Tina listened intently.

"Well, I learned that God made everything in the whole world, and I guess that's something I never knew. And I liked what you said, Reverend Brown, about Jesus loving everyone. I think I'd like to meet Jesus someday."

Karen looked at her husband, fighting back tears, realizing the importance of this tiny soul no one seemed to love.

Brent studied Tom for a long moment and felt something special stirring within the child's inner being. He knew for sure that this young boy could be trusted around his daughter.

"Tom," the pastor spoke softly, "we're mighty proud to have you as our guest, and I want you to know you are always welcome in our home."

Tom blushed and lowered his head. "Thank you, sir. I, uh … I really like it here."

"I told you he was a nice boy, Daddy," Tina said matter-of-factly.

"Yes you did, darling," Karen interjected. "And you were so right!"

"Daddy, can Thomas and I go out and play with Lady?"

"Sure you can, angel, and take her a big bowl of table scraps."

"Change out of your church clothes before you go out, Tina." Karen tried to suck the words back into her mouth, knowing that Tom probably didn't have much else to wear. Brent instantly saw Karen's *kick myself* expression.

"Tina, you go change; there's something I want to show Tom."

"Okay, Daddy. Don't leave, Tom!"

"I won't." Tom smiled down to his heart.

Reverend Brown and Thomas walked to the large out-building with the double wooden doors.

"You know, son, the Lord provides for all his children."

"I didn't know that, sir, but I believe you."

Brent smiled. "For the past several months, we've been collecting children's clothes from all over the county. People that have more than others should try to help the less fortunate. Do you understand what I'm saying?"

"Um, I think so sir. It's like when Tina tried to give me part of her lunch, but I was too embarrassed to take it."

"You are older than your years, Thomas Tabor, much older."

Tina came racing from the back kitchen door with her big, golden dog leaping joyfully alongside as her father and Tom exited the outbuilding.

Tina stopped in her tracks as Lady did a 360-degree turn in surprise. "Well then, Thomas Tabor, just where did you get new play clothes?"

"Um, well, Tina, your father—"

"It's the clothes we've been saving for the church family, little girl, and I guess Tom's part of that family now, right?"

Tina contemplated her father's words for a second. "Yeah, right, Daddy. He's part of the church family, our family, and my best friend!" Her giggle was infectious, as both the older man and young boy laughed with the little girl.

"Okay, kids." Brent bent over, placing his arms around their shoulders. "I'm going inside to read the Sunday paper. You guys can go play, but stay in sight, all right?"

"Yes, sir!" Tina snapped to attention, looking a lot like Shirley Temple in a toy soldier's uniform.

"Mr. Brown," Tom spoke nervously.

"Yes, son?"

"Can you see way up there on the hill where the four big pine trees are?"

"Yes, Tom, I can see the trees. What is it?"

"Well, sir, that's where my secret place is, and nobody I know has been there 'cept me. And all the wildflowers in the world grow there, and I promised Tina I'd show her, you know, for helping me on the bus, and uh, if you don't mind, sir ... "

Brent held up his hand in an understanding fashion, simply stating, "I understand, Tom. You can show Tina your secret place; just stay within sight and take Lady with you."

"Oh, thank you, Daddy!" The little girl hugged her father's neck.

"Mr. Brown?" Tom stood tightly as he solemnly spoke. "I'd never let anything happen to Tina."

Brent tilted his head to the side, contemplating such a bold, sincere statement. He saw maturity beyond years in the young lad before him. Smiling to himself, he turned toward the house as a tear trickled down his cheek.

Karen rocked slowly back and forth in the backyard glider as she read the book of James from the New Testament. She listened to the innocent laughter of the two children jumping merrily through the field of clover with the big yellow dog. As they approached the backyard, Brent also came outside, stretching his arms skyward and yawning like a big fat cat after a sound Sunday nap.

"Oh, Mommy, Mommy!" Tina's joy reached out for all to experience. "Thomas showed me the secret place, and there are so many flowers that we couldn't count them in a million years! It's so beautiful, Daddy!"

Tina held tightly to a full bouquet of lavender, yellow, red, and green flowers.

From behind his back, Tom produced an even larger arrangement of white, yellow, and ruby lilies, fidgeting as he held out his bouquet of love to Tina's mother.

"Lilies of the field," Karen whispered reverently.

"Thanks for having me to dinner and for taking me to church, Mrs. Brown."

The preacher's wife fell speechless.

Brent broke the peaceful silence. "You think your mother would allow you to go to church with us tonight, Tom?"

"Um, I kinda doubt it, sir. Um, Mom and, uh, Big Earl usually go out on Sunday night, and I need to take care of Baby."

"Baby?" Karen looked puzzled.

"Yes, ma'am, Baby. She's four years old, and uh, is real handicapped. I always take care of her when Mom is gone."

"Oh, I see." Karen wanted more than ever to hold and protect this child from what must be a horrible existence.

"Can I drive you home, son?"

"No thank you, sir. If I run, I'll be there before you can start the car."

Uneasy laughter did not diminish the sorrow Karen and Brent felt for this fragile, little boy with the big heart.

"Well, Tom, thanks for coming over." Brent reached out and shook the boy's hand like real men do.

"Will you go to church with us next Sunday, Tom?"

"Yes, ma'am, if'n I'm invited."

"You are, honey. Yes, you are always invited." Karen touched his smooth cheek tenderly.

"I'll see you on the way to school tomorrow, Thomas Tabor!" Tina gave him a quick peck on the cheek, and Tom's face went tulip red.

Tom turned and walked out through the clover and headed home. His gait quickened until he hit full stride. As the Browns reached the back door, Brent turned to see the boy leap into the air and heard a joyful "Yeehaw" before Tom disappeared behind the leafless, dark trees that guarded the Tabors' shack.

That evening, Tom slept more peacefully than he could ever remember. He did not awake at three a.m., nor did he wet himself that night or ever again.

The next morning, Thomas Lavon Tabor walked the muddy track to the main road, proudly wearing the clothes the pastor provided the previous day. He was smiling and quietly humming, "Jesus loves me, this I know."

The Letter: August 6

||||||||||||||||||||||||||||||||||||||||||||||||||||||||||||||||||||||||||

You know, Tina, I often wonder what my life might have been like had I been blessed with loving parents like yours.

Oh, I'm not looking for excuses for the evil I've done, and I don't buy the prison shrink's explanation about childhood pain and neglect. Lots of people grow up hard. As a mater of fact, I've met a lot of men inside and outside of this hellhole that would have loved to have grown up like I did. I guess no matter what your circumstance, it can always be worse.

Enough wishing I'd lived a better childhood. Let me get back to the sins of the past, beginning with the first one that started me down the road of no return.

Do you remember the time when we were in the fourth grade when the teacher brought me to the front of the class and whipped me until I cried because I fell asleep at my desk?

At recess that day, the taunting and shouts of "crybaby" made me truly wish I were dead. I ran from the playground vowing never to return to school. I can recall that moment as if it were only yesterday.

It began to rain as I walked the five-mile stretch from school to home. A nine-year-old kid should never have to face the humiliation, fear, and hopelessness I experienced that day.

By the time I reached the house, completely soaked by the cold rain, I began to shake as if I might just break apart. In reflection, I'm not sure if the cold rain brought on my convulsions or the sudden knowledge that death would be such a welcomed relief.

From a distance, I could see my old dog, Brown, slowly walking in the rain up our muddy driveway as if each step he took might be his last. The poor mutt was so old that most of his teeth were gone, and he could barely hear anything. I knew each step for him brought pain.

I stopped for a long moment, watching the aging dog, and began to cry as I saw how much Brown and me were alike. Stuck out in the rain, humiliated daily, and void of all hope and love.

And then, Tina, I committed my first unforgivable sin ...

The First Sin

||||||||||||||||||||||||||||||||||||||||||||||||||||||||||||||||||||||||||

Poke Tabor sped around the curve, downshifting the rusty Chevy with the souped-up motor into second gear. Coming from the opposite direction, he did not see his younger brother standing at the edge of the road in the pouring rain.

Poke cursed profusely as the Chevy's back end slid in the dark purple mud of the Tabor driveway. Shortly before leaving his job at Miller's Garage, the teenager washed, waxed, and thoroughly cleaned the inside of his most prized possession, a 1953, rust-covered Chevy with the inscription *Bad to the Bone* poorly painted across the trunk lid.

Poke didn't date often. As a matter of fact, he didn't date at all. Even in a country, one-horse town, boys with green teeth, cheap beer breath, and festering pimples could not even attract the ugliest girl to be found. But he'd gotten lucky this day, real lucky.

Mr. Miller couldn't say for sure if he liked the skinny, red-headed, dumb-as-a-brick teenager, but he did respect Poke's mechanical expertise.

Old man Miller was like most of the redneck hillbillies in the community of poverty and incestuous behavior. Work hard all day, drink all night, and have sex with anything that moved. His daughter, Uverna, would be no exception.

Uverna tested out with an IQ of just over eighty points. Short, fat, and what some would call smelly, the girl, like Poke, didn't have a lot of boys beating down the door asking for a date. She spent most waking hours sitting behind the heavy NCR cash register at her daddy's garage, eating Moonpies and Hostess Snowball Cupcakes. The old saying "opposites attract" did not apply in the budding relationship between Poke and Uverna.

A match made in heaven, some might think. Two peas in a pod, apples from the same tree, Jack Sprat and his mate, or the best characterization might be Stinky and Pinky.

Mr. Miller was no man's fool, and he peripherally watched his fat daughter and the bony, teenage grease monkey act like two dogs in heat each day, all day. He also knew that the chances of Uverna ever finding a husband were slim to none. Therefore, Poke had been given some consideration, even if only in Miller's secret thoughts, as potential husband material. That thought raced toward reality the night of Uverna's major announcement.

Mr. Miller's wife passed away when Uverna was but five years old. Semi-retarded, the young girl became the new target of abuse from her father—the same harsh verbal and physical kind that most likely killed her mother.

Mr. Miller finished counting the day's receipts as his daughter opened her eighth banana Moonpie of the day.

"Papa?" The girl's voice sounded nervous, although her father didn't notice. He grunted in response, licking his fingers as he counted out all the ones from the cash register.

"Papa, I, uh, ain't seen my time for I reckon two months now."

"Huh?" Mr. Miller once again grunted and spit a load of Red Man tobacco saliva toward the overweight greasy garage cat. "What the hell you talking 'bout, gal?"

"You know, Papa," she almost pleaded. "I ain't had my monthly time for two months!"

"Speak English, girl, before I box your ears!"

"Papa, I'm pregnant!" Her voice erupted, and the sobbing made her heft rock like scooped-out Jell-O.

Miller instantly turned beet red with anger, and the fact that he'd just swallowed a fist full of juicy Red Man tobacco only increased his fury.

"Why, you little whore," he hissed. "I'm gonna beat your fat ass black and blue!"

"I ain't no whore, Papa!" Uverna jumped to her feet to run as Miller loosened the buckle to his thick brown belt. "I swear, Papa, I ain't never been with no other man 'cept you."

Miller's anger quickly went south until it slammed head on with revulsion, and he suddenly felt like a rat caught in a jumbo trap with back legs paralyzed, clutching a chunk of molded cheese.

He thought for a moment. "Have you told anyone 'bout this? Tell me the truth, girl, or I'll kill you."

"No, Papa, I swear, only you. I've told only you."

"Okay, then." His simple, perverted mind began to click. "Here's what we're gonna do."

The next morning, Mr. Miller invited Poke for coffee across the street at The Ham and Eggs, an act that thoroughly surprised yet pleased the young man.

"You know, Poke, I've a been a watching you and my little girl of late. I think you got the hots for my baby."

Poke's blushing became so severe that even his pimples turned bright red.

"Oh, no, sir," he lied. "Why, Mr. Miller, I think Uverna is sweet and real pretty too, but no, sir, I wouldn't do anything that you didn't want me to."

"Now calm down, boy, calm down—I ain't mad at ya. Why, hell, I think you're a fine young man."

"Well, thanks a million, Mr. Miller," Poke answered, too stupid to even know what was coming.

"You know, boy, I ain't getting any younger, and someday, I'll want to retire and leave my business for my little girl."

Poke just shook his head dumbfounded like.

"And you know, boy, she ain't too smart. She's gonna need a real man to take care of her and to manage my garage. Are you listening, boy?"

"Um, yeah—I mean, yes, sir, Mr. Miller. I'm a listening. Um, what do you want me to do?"

"Take her out, boy! Are you stupid or something?"

"Um, no sir, I don't think so. Um, take her where?"

What a complete moron, Miller thought as he also recognized the perfect match between Poke and Uverna.

"Tell you what, Poke. I'm gonna give you the afternoon off, son, with pay! Now you go home, clean up, may be a good idea to buy a pint of Old Crow."

"Yes, sir." Poke could not fully grasp his good fortune.

"You come back to the garage, see, pick up Uverna, and take her home. I've got to work late, and this way you two can get to know each other better. How's that sound, boy?"

"Sounds like I'm the luckiest guy in the world, Mr. Miller."

Poke left the garage at half past one that day.

"Okay, Uverna, I've worked things through as to get you outta this mess. Now you better damn well do as I say, girl, cause Poke Tabor is soon goin' to be the daddy of that baby you're a carryin'."

Poke could not be completely sure what old man Miller had proposed, but whatever the case, he planned to have one hell of a good time with Uverna that day.

Tom screamed out in anguish as his brother laid on the Chevy's horn, and old Brown walked slowly through the mud in front of the car, not hearing the horn or Tom's pleading for the dog to run.

Anger built, and Poke's motivation to get to Uverna as soon as possible got the better of him. Mud flew as the Chevy fishtailed left and right with the gas pedal touching the floorboard.

Tom clearly heard the two thumps of the front and back right-side tires, and the final yelp from the old dog that had provided the only moments of affection for him in the Tabor household.

Tom charged forward in fury and panic, throwing himself in the mud, pulling Brown's big neck to his chest.

"Please, God, don't take Brown," he moaned. "Please, God—Brown's all I got!"

His prayer went unanswered, and the boy wept like his heart would explode as he lovingly carried the big dog into the knee-high weeds along the muddy road.

The boy cried himself dry and felt his sorrow transform to uncontrollable anger.

"I'm gonna kill you, Poke."

"What the hell you doing home, turd face?" Poke asked as Tom stood silently watching his older brother brush his slimy teeth with salt and baking soda.

"Where you goin', Poke?" Tom's voice scratched with subdued hatred.

"None of your damn business, Pee Baby—that's where I'm going." Poke laughed sarcastically and grimaced as he splashed Old Spice on his newly squeezed pimples.

"You seen Brown today, Poke?"

"Huh?" Poke hesitated. "Hell no, I ain't seen that mutt. Probably crawled off and died if we're lucky."

"Yeah?" Tom's smile portrayed a newly acquired evil. "Seen your wallet and your whiskey bottle, Poke?"

"What the—" Poke turned to see his little brother's face twisted in a grotesque expression. Tom held his arms out, holding his brother's tattered wallet in one hand and the pint of Old Crow Whiskey in the other.

"You killed my dog, Poke. Now I'm going to throw your wallet and whiskey in the pond."

"Why, you little asshole!" Poke jumped at Tom, tripping on the chrome kitchen chair as he hit the greasy floor hard. "I'm gonna kill you!"

Tom bolted for the outside as Poke scurried to his feet, racing to the door in outrage and panic.

"Come here, you little turd!" Poke screamed as Tom hit the edge of the woods with speed and agility.

Tom had found the cave the previous summer while he and Brown romped along the edge of his secret, special place. The boy had gone there that day for the sole purpose of picking flowers for Tina and her mother. Brown jumped a ground squirrel and chased the speedy, little critter into an enormous thicket of honeysuckle and blackberry bushes.

Tom could hear his dog barking like a coonhound with a treed possum, but his yapping seemed distant and muffled. After crawling, pulling, and becoming totally entangled in briers, Tom looked on in amazement at the large hole cut out of the rocky hillside behind the thicket.

The boy followed Brown's growling through the large opening, moving cautiously as he attempted to adjust his focus in the nearly pitch black, damp environment.

About five feet in, Tom reached out for Brown, who seemed to be blocking the boy from going any further. The outside light provided just enough of an aura for Tom to see the large opening in the ground just inside the cave's small entrance. He pushed a handful of loose dirt and rock into the hole. It seemed to take forever before the pebbles hit bottom.

Tom quickly left the cave with Brown in tow, returning the next day with dog and kerosene lantern for further exploration.

Tom estimated that the inside of his new secret place had to be just about twice the size of the school gym. His discovery was indeed a special event in his life.

About six feet inside the entrance was the hole, some four feet across. On each side, Tom found a well-worn pathway, three feet across. Inside, the ceiling rose nearly twenty feet, and the rock and clay walls were covered with magnificent drawings. Along the floor of the cave, the boy gathered arrow-heads, clay pots, and other items not easily identified. Yes, Tom and Brown had indeed found a magical, secret place, and the boy never told a soul about it, not even Tina, his best friend.

Poke, now totally engulfed in rage, knew for sure he would beat Tom within an inch of his life. From the corner of his right eye, he caught a glimpse of the boy running across the field toward the large, steep hill.

"You're trapped now, you little bastard," Poke hissed venomously.

"Tom! Hey, little brother!" Poke attempted to sound sincere. "I'll give you two dollars if you'll come back, Tom. I swear I won't hit you or nothing!"

He couldn't be sure if his brother heard his pleadings. A moment later, from across the meadow, Tom's reply echoed. "Screw you, Poke—you killed my dog. Come and get me, murderer!"

"You're dead now," Poke stated with certainty.

The rain continued to fall in heavy sheets, and Poke cursed as he realized his best clothes would not be what he was wearing for his date with Uverna. He crossed the meadow, standing near the spot he'd last seen his brother.

"Come on, Tom, I'm beggin' ya. I've got a big date tonight, and look, you're screwing it all up."

"You killed Brown, Poke." Tom's voice sounded muffled.

"Where the hell are you?" Poke shouted as he crawled through the thicket of briers, following Tom's distant voice.

"I'm in here, pimple face!" Tom's laughter gave Poke chills.

Poke found the opening, pushed his shoulders through, and listened for any sound. Then he heard a match being struck and watched as Tom lit the kerosene lantern, standing some distance away toward the back of what appeared to be a large cave.

Tom almost sounded like he was growling as he invitingly held out the wallet and whiskey. "Come and get it, pimple face."

"You're mine now!" Poke jumped to a standing position with shoulders slumped over and charged straight ahead.

As if caught in a nightmare, Poke's fourth step found open air, and he fell into ebony nothingness for what seemed like an eternity. Tom barely heard the thump as his brother lay bashed and broken at the bottom of the pit.

"Help me, Tom! Oh please, God help me! I think my legs are broken." The painful, pleading echo did nothing to erase the hatred Tom felt.

Tom leaned over the deep hole, holding the lantern above it. He could just barely make out the shadow of his broken brother.

Poke coughed hard as pain gripped his every movement, and blood poured out his mouth and nose.

"Help me, Tom—please help me," he whimpered.

"See Brown today, Poke?" Tom extinguished the lantern, crawled out, and carefully placed large rocks across the cave's entrance.

Returning home, the boy immediately went to the storage shed behind the Tabor shack, digging through all the junk until he located the wheel barrel with the front steel wheel and a badly rusted shovel. Tom dug for nearly two hours until the hole overlooking the meadow of flowers was large enough for Brown. He gently lowered his companion in the hole on top of Poke's wallet and bottle of whiskey. Tom then spent another hour collecting large rocks, covering the mound of mud that forever concealed his dog … and the evidence of his first sin.

It was nearly a week before Mr. Miller talked to the sheriff regarding the whereabouts of Poke Tabor.

"I need to find that boy, Sheriff," old man Miller had stated remorsefully. "That no good Tabor boy done knocked up my little girl!"

Sheriff Hightower did stop by the Tabors' shack and inquired about the missing Poke two days later.

"How the hell should I know where the moron is?" Big Earl responded.

"You know, Sherrell," the sheriff spoke nervously. "Mr. Miller says his daughter is with child and Poke's the daddy!"

"Mom," Tom spoke up. "A couple a weeks ago when I got home from school, I saw Poke get in a car with a couple a strangers. They seemed to be in a real hurry and kinda drunk too."

Sherrell shook her head in disgust. "Well there you go, Sheriff. Just another dirt bag running out on his kid."

"Good riddance," Big Earl added, belched, and emptied the remaining foam from his beer.

"Well, maybe he'll be back someday," the sheriff said in passing.

"Bet he won't," Tom whispered and walked out the door.

The Letter: August 7

|||||||||||||||||||||||||||||||||||||||||||||||||||||||||||||||||

Shortly after Poke's disappearance, or some might say demise, things just kept going downhill in a hurry.

I tried to be a good person, Tina, but the evil that surrounded me was constant and too much for any young kid to run from.

When I think back to that period of time, it seems like I lived two separate lives. Six days a week I was humiliated, tortured, hungry, and neglected in every way. Then there was Sunday. For half a day each week, I felt love. Your parents were so kind, and learning about Jesus even brought me hope; and of course, there you were, the love of my life.

But try to imagine a living hell except for a short period each week. That was my life back then, Tina.

The only thing that kept me from not jumping into the pit with Poke was the daily trip on the bus to and from school. You *always saved a seat for me and defended me against the multitude of hateful kids that found such delight in my humiliation.*

I reckon one of my most painful memories occurred the last day of school in the fourth grade. You were so happy! Remember showing me your report card? All A's, and the big black stamp across the middle, "Passed to the Fifth Grade." I remember your words clear as a bell. "Oh, Thomas, won't it be fun to be in the fifth grade together?" You were always so full of hope and cheerfulness, my precious Tina.

I could not bring myself to tell you the truth. My level of humiliation found the very bottom that day. I walked off that bus and ran non-stop to the secret place like a wild animal. I tore through the briers, threw the rocks aside like a crazy person, and entered the darkness of my mystical cave.

I sat in the blackness and wept so hard that my body actually ached from the repetitive shuddering. I reached into my coat pocket and pulled the Zippo lighter I had stolen from Poke and watched the yellow flame as one might see hell from a thousand miles away. Then from my other coat pocket, I pulled out the report card and read, "Failed. Report to Fourth Grade." I dropped the yellow card into the hole with what remained of Poke's bones.

Now all the kids could add "stupid" and "retarded" to the list of Thomas Tabor's attributes. But that didn't bother me near as much as realizing you would be leaving me behind.

I don't know how long I remained in the secret place, but when I crawled out, the sky grew black, almost evil, and coldness went through me like what lost souls must experience the moment before they enter eternity.

I walked home, not remembering a single step, and that same day, I committed the second sin.

The Second Sin

||||||||||||||||||||||||||||||||||||||||||||||||||||||||||

The blackness of the night gave the shack the appearance of something dark and evil. Tom shivered as he felt a prevailing spirit move through the trees surrounding the desolate house that warned him that something truly wicked awaited.

His fear intensified by the fact that no light illuminated from the shack. The interior looked even darker than the gloom surrounding the tomb he called home.

"Baby," Tom whispered. "Oh my God, what's happened to Baby?"

Concern for his helpless sister dissipated the foreboding fear momentarily. Tom rushed into the shack, groping in the darkness for the string that hung from the center of the room that, once pulled, might drive the sinister evil from the house.

The tiny bell at the string's end sounded to Tom like music from hell. With a trembling hand, he reached out, found the string, and pulled. The forty-watt bulb exploded into light upon the greasy kitchen table covered with four days' worth of dirty dishes. He immediately saw the note in the middle, secured by an empty beer can.

Tom,

Mom and Big Earl went to Huntington for the weekend. I'm going to Gina's and will be home Sunday so you can go to church. Take care of Baby.

Love ya, Doral

"Baby!" Tom screamed as he returned to the urgency before him. "Baby!" He ran through the stained pink sheet covering the entrance to his mother's bedroom, ripping it from the silver thumbtacks holding it in place.

Tom found the wooden lamp made to look like a well pump and turned on the yellow bug light. "Oh, Baby, sweet Baby," the boy moaned.

His baby sister lay uncovered in the too-small crib, wearing nothing but a diaper that had not been changed for what he surmised to be at least ten hours.

Tom quickly pulled the spread from his mother's bed, wrapping it tightly around Baby, pulling her to his chest.

"I'm here, Baby. I'm here, little one. Tom will take care of you."

The young child's skin felt clammy and cold as ice. Tom realized that no one thought to light the kerosene heater, and the inside temperature must be below fifty degrees.

"Assholes," Tom said with true hatred and laid Baby on the bed as he lit the heater.

The boy gagged in violent heaves as he attempted to change his helpless sister's diaper. Tom froze in place as Baby began to convulse, and her big, beautiful, sky-blue eyes rolled back in her head, out of sight. A nine-year-old boy hopelessly alone could not be expected to handle such an immediate peril.

Tom ran into the living room, snatching the black handset phone.

"Oh, yes, Myrtle, I think you're so right, you know. The Tompkins just think they're so much better than everybody else!"

The Tabors shared the Ma Bell party line with three other phone customers.

Tom, breathing in gasps, interrupted. "Please, hang up right now—Baby's sick real bad!"

"Who is this?" Myrtle Watkins shot back with great indignation. "Can't you see we're having a conversation here?"

"Yes," the other old biddy chimed in. "Hang up, or I'll report you to the operator!"

Tom's voice went low and filled the phone line with vicious terror. "Hang the phone up now, or I swear I'll burn your houses down!"

The phone lines went dead, and Tom called the operator. "Oh, God, please call the sheriff! Baby's dying. I need help!"

"Sorry, sir, that line is busy. Please try again later."

Tom slammed the phone down hard, causing the cheap glass figurines his mother cherished to fall to the floor and break into a thousand tiny pieces of glittering nothingness.

Racing back into his mother's bedroom, Tom returned to the crib, finding Baby ghostly white. The poor, neglected child's eyes now looked directly up into Tom's face. Her grunts and groans reminded Tom of the pleadings from a dying animal. It was almost as if he heard her saying, "Please let me die, Tom. I want to go see Jesus."

Tom wept without sound as he held the small pillow over Baby's mouth and nose. "I love you, Baby." He sobbed. "You've suffered long enough. It's time to go to a better place, Baby. Forgive me, Baby, I love you."

Baby's eyes grew crystal clear and peaceful. When he lifted the pillow, the innocent child wore a smile upon her tiny face.

The gossiping hens were not on the line, and the phone only rang twice before Tom heard, "Sheriff's department."

Tom did not go to church that Sunday. Instead he watched silently as the Reverend Brown performed the funeral service for Baby Tabor.

Doral did not return that Sunday morning as promised, and Sherrell would not be home until the following Wednesday.

The only people attending the funeral for Baby Tabor were Tom, Reverend and Mrs. Brown, Tina, and old man Winn, who listened to Tom's heartfelt pleas before donating a quarter acre of land he owned that overlooked the special place of a thousand flowers. That small parcel of land became Baby's final destination upon earth.

The Letter: August 8

Doral arrived home late Sunday night and only asked if Mom had come back. I guess she was worried about Mom finding out she'd been gone all weekend.

"What about Baby?" I asked her. "Don't you care about your sister?"

"Huh?" Doral answered. "Oh, yeah, sure I do, little brother. How is Baby?"

"She's dead," I told her.

I took Doral to the grave, and she just stared down at the dirt hump I'd surrounded with white creek stones. She didn't shed a tear or say a word, but I knew her heart was broken. I think Doral believed she'd caused Baby's death. For a moment, I almost told her the truth. I almost told her that I sent Baby to be with Jesus, but I thought better of it. Now, only you and God know the truth.

When my mom and Big Earl finally came home, still drunk, I took them to the grave. Mamma fell on the ground and rolled around, screaming like she just might have gone crazy.

For sure she thought Baby's death was her fault, and I wanted her to. Mom changed that day and seemed to go into a darkness no one could reach beyond and pull her out of. Maybe God thought it was payback time for neglecting little Baby all those years.

I will give Big Earl a little credit, though. He did build a nice white fence around the plot of land where both Baby and Brown were buried. He left plenty of space for additional graves 'cause Mamma said that's where she wanted to be laid to rest. I reckon that's the last place I want to go, before I travel on to hell.

I missed you so much that summer, but I just couldn't find the will to face you and your parents. I wanted to forget about God, hope, love, and all those things your daddy talked about in church. They might have been true where you lived, but when you crossed the field and walked into the Tabor yard, you sure as heck weren't going to find God or anything else one might consider good.

That entire summer, I spent every day alone in the cave, studying the carvings some long-ago Indians had drawn. Beautiful things they were. You could see mighty battles, hunters standing over wild beasts they killed, and brave warriors upon their powerful horses. There were pictures of the sun and moon. Pictures of what looked like stars streaking across the sky. But the best of all these drawings stood at the back wall, rising nearly fifteen feet. It was placed, I came to realize, in such a position that at midday the sun shone through the tiny crack in the ceiling rock and rays of light illuminated the drawing so it could be seen clearly, even when no other light existed in the cave. The drawing was of a cross with a man hanging lifeless-like upon it. He looked like he wore a bunch of thorns on his head. Above his head, the letters Y-A-H-W-E-H were cut in stone.

The only peace I found during that lonely summer was at the foot of that drawing.

As the summer ended, my panic level accelerated. I didn't really care anymore about the other kids making fun of me. As a matter of fact, I almost looked forward to it. If you recall, I grew a lot that year, and a special feeling seemed to build inside me. Just let one boy call me stupid or retarded, and I knew I would beat the living hell out of him. So my panic no longer came from the other children's taunting; it came from the fear of losing you.

I remember how cold that first day of school was and couldn't figure out why I kept sweating like I'd run five miles. Now I know. I worried if somebody else would be sitting next to the only love I knew.

Like always, though, you were true to form.

"Hey, Thomas Tabor! I've been saving a seat for you!"

Your voice melted every fear and black thought from my mind. If you still liked me, I thought, I could endure anything.

I tried hard that year. I guess I was stupid enough to believe that if I studied, did my homework, and kept my mouth shut in class, just maybe somehow I could get pushed up to the fifth grade with you.

That Thanksgiving, Mom had been in the hospital for a nervous breakdown for nearly a month. Big Earl stayed drunk waiting for his trial for car theft, and Doral quit school to take care of things while Mamma recovered.

Big Earl found lots of reasons to beat me almost daily. That was okay—I could handle it. But once again, the feeling of evil crept back into our existence, and Big Earl looked and acted more like the devil himself with each passing day.

The night before his trial, he got especially violent, and his expressions seemed so terribly evil that for the first time, I feared for my life.

Doral came home around midnight after going out on a date with Johnny Boy Hayburn, a nice guy, as I recall.

I remained quiet and motionless in the dark living room, terrified of Big Earl's drunken fury. I heard him pop the top to a fresh beer and stumble from the kitchen as Doral walked into the house. By daylight, I would have finalized my third sin ...

The Third Sin

||||||||||||||||||||||||||||||||||||||||||||||||||||||||||||||||||

"Hey, you little whore." Big Earl slurred his every word. "Your mamma's in the hospital, and I ain't had no supper! What the hell's the matter with you?"

Tom could physically feel Doral's terror.

"Oh gosh, Earl, I'm sorry, would you like some biscuits and eggs? I'll fix 'em in a jiff."

The big man scratched his ever-growing beer belly and laughed sinisterly as he put both his fat arms against the wall, pinning Doral in between. She almost gagged as his putrid breath engulfed her in the stale air of the Tabor shack.

"Yeah, you little tease, I might just want me a big breakfast after I works me up an appetite." His left hand moved swiftly down to Doral's blue jeans, painfully squeezing her buttocks.

"But first I think I'd like a little taste of what you've been giving that hillbilly Johnny Boy."

"Oh no, Earl, please don't do this—I'm begging you!"

Earl's rough, two-day-old beard scratched at Doral's face as he opened his mouth, showing his tobacco-stained teeth.

"Let's just have a little kiss, darling, and Big Earl will show you what a real man's got!"

"No, Earl, no! I swear I'll tell Mamma."

Earl backhanded Doral, breaking her nose in the process. "You ain't tellin' nobody nothin', you little whore! Now get out of those britches before I give ya what for!"

Earl tore Doral's blouse from her body as he ripped her bra in half, exposing her small breasts. Slapping her in the face again, his bloodshot eyes bulged like those of a lunatic.

"Now get your whorin' ass into that bed, girl, before I kill you!"

Doral slumped to the floor, choking back sobs of pure terror, attempting to cover her nakedness with frail arms.

Tom ran into the room from behind, jumping on Big Earl's back, screaming as he clawed at the drunken assailant's eyes.

"Leave her alone, you bastard, or I'll kill you!"

Earl easily threw Tom into the icebox, hard. The boy's head hit the solid metal surface and a thousand stars appeared before the blackness fell.

"You've had it now, you little bitch—play time is over!" Saliva secreted from the corners of Earl's lips, and pure unadulterated evil permeated from his presence. He literally threw Doral across the room onto the bed.

The terrified girl rolled onto her stomach as Earl pulled and tugged at her blue jeans while also pulling his pants to his knees.

Tom reached behind his head and felt the ooze of blood.

He snarled the words, "I'm gonna kill you tonight, Big Earl."

Tom found the Louisville Slugger behind the icebox and moved quietly to the side of the big man as he began to crawl on his sister.

"Hey, Earl, you piece of shit!" Tom hissed.

Earl turned around just in time to catch Tom's full blow of the bat upon his crotch, sending the man to his knees in never-before-experienced anguish.

"Ahhh!" he cried out in unbearable pain. "I'm going to kill you, you little bastard!"

"Not today!" Tom shot back. The baseball bat once again struck Earl—flush in the face, knocking out eight teeth in the process. Earl fell sideways, clutching his now toothless mouth with one hand and his broken penis with the other.

"Run, Doral, run!" Tom reached out to the bedside table and tossed Doral Big Earl's car keys. "Go get help, sis—go get help!"

Doral ran into the living room, grabbing her raincoat to cover her nakedness. Within seconds, she tore down the muddy driveway in Earl's stolen red Caddy.

"You ain't so big now, are you, Big Earl?" Tom spit in the fat man's face and whacked him good in the ribs.

"You're dead meat, you little bastard," Earl moaned through bloody lips.

"Come and get me, pervert! Come and get me!"

Tom ran to the front door, snatching the flashlight off the coffee table as he exited.

"I'm coming, boy! I'm sure as hell coming for you!" Big Earl painfully rose, pulled up his pants, moaning as he slid his dirty feet into the lace-less rubber boots. He tapped against his right pants pocket to make sure the four-inch Hook-bill knife was still there. "I'm coming, boy, and I'm gonna cut your heart out!"

Earl fell down the loose, rotting steps and painfully sprawled out in the dew-covered front yard. From thirty feet away, the white light shone in his eyes, and the boy's reflection stood taunting behind it.

"Here I am, pervert—come get me!"

Earl grunted, pushed himself up from the ground, and staggered in the direction of the light.

The overweight drunk huffed and puffed as he followed the swaying flashlight toward the meadow where Baby had been buried.

"Where the hell you taking me, boy?" He pulled and opened the big Hook-bill knife. "Ah shit!" Earl said in recognition of the sound of police sirens no doubt meant for him. "Screw it! I'm going to kill you, Tommy Boy!" His powerful voice echoed through the valley.

"Over here, Big Earl," Tom taunted the man. "Does your tiny pecker hurt, Big Earl?" Earl growled and found new energy as he semi-sprinted twenty yards to the thicket where the flickering light stopped moving forward.

The fury overwhelmed the man as he crashed into the bushes like a wounded water buffalo.

"I'm going to kill you!" His rage uncontrollable now, he slashed away at the clinging thorns and briers with his knife.

He saw the light inside a strange opening. All logic long gone and replaced with driving rage, Big Earl dove head first into the cave, crawling with pure malice and deadly intent.

Big Earl stopped as the cave suddenly brightened toward the back. He watched as Tom slowly walked toward him, swinging a lantern in a carefree manner.

"Hey there, Big Earl, the crybaby. Did a little boy kick your butt?"

The noise that came out did not sound like anything human, as the bull of a man charged the boy, slashing the air violently with his knife.

His right foot found the pit first, followed immediately by the left. His forward motion pushed his hands beyond the hole, and Earl clung to the edge, digging his fingers into the hard dirt.

"Oh God, oh God—please help me!" Earl pleaded like a terrified child.

"Oh God?" Tom laughed. "You know God, Big Earl? I don't think so."

Tom placed the sole of his shoe on Earl's fat fingers, grinding them into the rocky soil.

"Please, Tom! I'm sorry; don't let me die! I'm beggin' ya!"

Tom raised his leg high and gave a tremendous final stomp on Earl's bleeding hand. His falling scream bounced off the cave walls like shrieks from hell.

"Nighty-night, Big Earl." Tom's grin was anything but that of a child. "Say hello to Poke while you're down there!"

Earl knew his back was broken. He frantically reached out in all directions as if looking for something to cling to in this pit of eternal damnation.

"What?" he moaned, spitting up great amounts of blood. He felt something smooth and round. Holes, yes; and bones. His agonized scream filled the air as he realized he was holding Poke's skull.

Tom casually walked into the front yard from the opposite direction of his secret place. The sheriff's car and the three deputies' blue lights gave a warm glow to the Tabors' dismal surroundings.

"Oh, Tom!" Doral ran sobbing to her brother, pulling him tightly into her arms. "You saved my life, Tom; you saved me, Tom!"

"Are you okay, boy?" The sheriff shined his huge black flashlight over the boy's entire body, now covered in mud.

"Yes, sir, I'm fine now, I think."

"Where did Big Earl run to, boy?"

"Well, sir, he chased me to the highway, waving his knife and swearing to kill me. I crawled down into the ditch and seen him run down the road like a crazy man until he plum disappeared. When I saw your lights, I knew you wouldn't let him hurt me and Doral no more."

"That's right, son. You're safe now."

Tom looked up, giving Doral a confident smile.

The sheriff turned to his number one deputy. "All right, Burns, call the state boys right away. Put out an APB on Earl Ray. Tell 'em he's wanted for car theft and, uh, attempted rape. Tell the state boys to be careful now; the man is armed and dangerous!"

"Not anymore," Tom spoke confidently in a mere whisper. "Not anymore."

Doral wondered what he meant but strangely knew not to ask.

The Letter: August 9

||||||||||||||||||||||||||||||||||||||||||||||||||||||||||||||||||||||

Big Earl was pretty well forgotten, and everyone in the county thought it was good riddance. Mamma came back home from the hospital a completely different person. She looked like a ghost. I don't think she missed Earl and most likely didn't much give a damn that Poke had also vanished. That might have been different if she'd known I killed him. But I really think Mamma mourned for Baby. That kind of guilt ain't easy to let go of.

I too often look deep inside and try hard to find feelings of guilt. I'm a little sorry about Poke, but not much. Big Earl deserved to die, and I remain pleased with myself for doing him in. Baby, I'm not yet sure how to feel about. The poor thing really had no life to speak of, and that would not have changed as she got older. Besides, she looked up at me before I put the pillow over her face, and I swear she was pleading with me to end her suffering. I guess I *mostly believe I did the right thing when I ended her agony and hopelessness.*

In keeping with my promise to continue to read the Bible you gave me each day, I gave up on The Old Testament, just too hard for this old dummy to comprehend. Now I'm reading in Matthew and must admit I feel peacefulness whenever I read the words in red.

It's hard to believe but certainly an accomplishment when you begin to realize just what Jesus did.

I think I'm right that he only walked around talking to people about three or four years. It wasn't a very big area that he traveled, either. And man, what a bunch of nobodies he led around! But he always did good things, wonderful things, and never asked any man for nothing. And what did he get for all that good, Tina? A big, fat nothing! They beat him, treated him worse than a dog. That wasn't good enough, though. Can you imagine being nailed to a cross and still asking God to forgive them that did that to you? Maybe he is the Son of God—I just don't know.

It's funny, now that I've been reading about Jesus, my memory went back to the secret place for the first time in many a year . . .

The Secret Place: Last Visit

IIIIIIIIIIIIIIIIIIIIIIIIIIIIIIIIIIIIIIIIIIIIIIIIIIIIIIIIIIIIIII

"Mamma, can I get you something to eat? Would you like some Kool-Aid and vanilla wafers?"

"No, thank you, honey." Sherrell's voice sounded as if she spoke from an endless void.

"You better hurry up and get ready, Tom. You might miss the bus."

"Yessum," Tom said politely. "I'll be home by three, Mamma."

Sherrell did not acknowledge her son. She curled up into the fetal position and silently drifted off into a troubled sleep filled with the ever-present terror that always crept into her dreams.

As was the case every day for the past three months, Tom climbed the huge oak tree at the edge of the woods and quietly watched the school bus make its way past the muddy Tabor driveway, disappearing around the bend of the curving black-top country road.

Tom knew that Tina would not be on the bus. She would be sitting beside Michael Klansky in his yellow 1955 Chevy. The only person Tom ever loved was now in the eleventh grade, while Tom would have been in the ninth grade for the second year.

Nobody at the school cared that Thomas Lavon Tabor didn't attend anymore. Truth be told, the principal, teachers, and the boys' counselor were actually happy. After all, all he did was beat up the other boys and disrupt every class he entered. Most thought Tom might be slightly retarded, although he wasn't. The misery, torture, and humiliation of his sixteen years on earth had taken a serious toll on the young man. Thomas Tabor could be considered soulless. He no longer experienced hate, anger, or much of anything else. And most assuredly, he did not experience love, except when he thought about Tina.

Tom spent most of his days walking and hitchhiking his way to Whitey's Pool Hall, some five miles from the Tabor shack. It was there that he would shoot pool with the local worthless drunks while guzzling Pabst Blue Ribbon beer until it was time to return home and take care of his mom.

The teenager's talent with a pool cue became legendary, and he would pocket four or five dollars every day before returning to the dismal existence of the Tabor family dwelling.

His sister Doral married Johnny Hayburn, and they moved to Kentucky after Johnny Boy got a good job at Ashland Oil Company. The couple named their son Thomas Paul Hayburn after Tom.

Doral visited six months earlier and brought her baby son along. Sherrell remained curled in a ball, heavily drugged with nerve medicine and did not even know Doral had been there.

"He sure is a handsome little guy, sis!"

"Yeah, he is a pretty thing, ain't he? Here, Tom, hold him." Doral placed the beautiful little guy in Tom's arms.

"I named him after you, little brother."

"Yeah? Well I'll be dropped in the mud. I never had nobody think enough about me to do something like that."

"Tom." Doral's eyes clouded with tears. "You saved my life. If it weren't for you, I'd been raped and probably killed. I want my baby to grow up to be like you."

Tom did not respond; he couldn't. Hard as he might try, there were no emotions to draw out. The boy just looked at his sister with near unbearable pain and quietly stated, "I did what I had to do, sis."

"Tom?"

"Yeah, sis?"

"What happened to Big Earl? I still have dreams he'll come back for me."

Tom stared at Doral for a long moment. "Trust me, Doral, he won't ever come back."

Doral reached out with her left hand, gently touching her brother's cheek. "Thank you, Tom," she whispered, knowing that the dreams could cease and also knowing her baby brother was most likely a murderer.

"I won't be back again, Tom. There's nothing here I wish to remember. Would you like to come live with us?"

"Nah, Doral, I best stay here and take care of Mom."

Doral's look said it all. She turned, leaving the dark memories of the Tabor family behind. Tom wept not knowing why as Doral drove down the muddy road for the final time.

The next day, Tom walked with his head bent low and the collar of the flimsy nylon jacket pulled high around his neck. The temperature, just above freezing, seemed to chill the boy clear to the bone as the sleet intensified. Tom did not hear the car approach.

"Can I give you a lift, son?" The cheerful voice sounded familiar.

Tom breathed a sigh of relief. "I'd surely appreciate a ride." Tom suddenly stopped as he peered through the passenger's window.

"Well, I'll be! Tom Tabor! Come on, son, get in. The weather's getting worse by the second."

Tom did not have a choice. "Thanks," Tom almost mumbled. "Good to see you again, Reverend Brown."

"Same here, boy, same here! So tell me, how have you been doing?"

"Good as expected, sir. You know, just taking each day as it comes."

Reverend Brown not only heard the pain in the boy's voice; he could feel it. The preacher fought to find the right words to say.

"It's been a while since we've seen you in church, Tom. You know, we have a great youth group now—some really wonderful young people. Why don't you come visit this Saturday? We're having a sixteenth birthday party for Tina. I'm sure she'd love to see you again." Brent Brown immediately wished he'd kept his mouth shut.

"Thank you, sir, but I've already got a commitment Saturday." The reverend knew that probably was not the case.

"Well, son, just know you're welcome at our church and our home anytime."

"Thanks, Reverend Brown. How's Tina?"

"Uh, great, son. You know, just a busy teenager always running here and there. Don't you see her at school?"

"No, sir." There was a painful pause. "We're in different classes now."

The preacher wanted to bite his tongue again. *You big dummy,* he thought. Of course, Tina had mentioned that Tom kept being set back in school.

"This is good, sir. You can let me out right here."

Tom quickly opened the car door to leave but stopped as he turned back to face the minister.

"You know, sir, you and Mrs. Brown are really wonderful people. I'll never forget how kind you were. Say hello to Tina for me." Tom quickly left before he exploded.

The Reverend Brown watched in hopelessness as Tom entered Whitey's Pool Hall. "Please keep your hand on that boy, dear Lord."

Tom rose early the following Sunday morning. He stood looking out across the yard from the back door. The sun seemed to fill the space with a soft glow as the dew-covered grass sparkled like a field of tiny diamonds. He watched several rather fat robins hop their way around finding big, juicy worms at will. Tom, surprised, realized he was smiling.

Tom felt different this sunny morning. He couldn't explain it, but he knew it was similar to the long-ago days when he'd eagerly awaited the Browns' automobile to arrive. Yes, to arrive and take him to church, to arrive and take him to the wonderful fried chicken, mashed potatoes, thick milk gravy, and homemade apple pie. To arrive and take him to Tina, the only person Tom could ever love.

Smiling like a happy child, Tom walked into his mother's bedroom, where she lay facing him in a distorted fashion.

"Mom, can I get you anything?" He spoke softly. "Are you okay?"

Sherrell did not respond. "I think I'll go to church today, Mom."

His mother simply grunted, turned her back in his direction, and once again curled up into a tight ball.

Tom walked away in silence, wishing he could summon some kind of feeling for his mother. Nothing. No hate, no anger, no disgust, no nothing. He cleaned up his ankle-high lace-up boots and carefully ironed his only decent shirt.

His smile returned as he envisioned the possibilities of a new day, maybe even a new beginning. Tom cut across the field of clover that separated the Tabor shack from the beautiful, white home with pale yellow shutters where the Browns resided. He walked their gravel driveway to the paved road and could see the church resting peacefully upon the hill.

"I love you, Tina," Tom whispered as hope resurrected in his heart. Thomas Tabor did not know this was Easter Sunday.

As he grew nearer the church, his joy retreated and panic took over.

"Just look at you!" he hissed. "Look at your clothes, your old, worn-out boots. You look like a bum, Tom Tabor! And a stupid bum at that!"

"Yeah, Tina will say, 'Oh, there you are, Thomas Tabor! I've been saving a seat just for you. I very much want to sit next to a ninth grader!'"

Tom did not enter the church. He instead hid himself in the parking lot until the doors were closed and the singing began. He bent low, quietly working his way through the cars until he stood below the long windows of the east wall of the church. Tom slowly slid his back down the wood boards until he rested on a grassy spot.

"What a friend we have in Jesus, all our burdens will he bear . . ."

Tom carefully listened to every word of that song and also to the sermon concerning all that Jesus Christ gave and suffered through for each living soul. That beautiful, bright sunny morning, Tom sincerely wished he could find Jesus.

After altar call, he once again moved quickly through the parking lot until he reached the safety of the tree line. From there, he could easily see the members file out the double doors and head home.

Yes, head home, he thought. Head home to love, a big dinner, to a peacefulness he'd never experienced.

Tom sucked in his breath in trepidation as Tina almost danced out the front door of the church, wearing a white, starched, cotton dress with creamy-white, patent-leather flats. The pink, silk bows in her gleaming blonde hair added to the completeness of the angelic figure reflecting in Tom's eyes. He wanted to cry out, to run to her. He needed for Tina to know that he loved her more than life itself. Then he staggered back, placing his hand tightly over his mouth, holding back his screams of desperation.

Tina laughed, joyfully bouncing into the yellow Chevy convertible next to Michael Klansky. Tom choked and sobbed as Klansky slipped his arm around Tina's shoulders and drove away.

Tom returned home, taking the long way through the woods. Walking through the tiny house, he quietly checked on his mother. She had not moved from the position he last saw her in.

Quickly going to the shed, now teetering on collapse at any moment, Tom found both a shovel and a pick axe. As if each step caused him pain, he shuffled up beyond the field of wildflowers toward the secret place. He did not notice the meadow in full bloom or the graves of Baby and Brown.

Crawling through the small cave opening, Tom reached out to his left. Finding the kerosene lantern, Tom struck a kitchen match and instantly brought the cavern into brightness. Walking past the pit where Big Earl and Poke now resided, Tom moved with purpose to the back wall. He had to see it one last time.

Tom stood before the high drawing of what he felt sure was that of Jesus Christ at his crucifixion. All thoughts of the day's previous events were gone. Only one thought remained.

"Are you here, Jesus?" Tom pleaded. "Where are you, Jesus? Can you hear me? Do you see me? Do you love me, Jesus?"

The ray of sunlight broke through the tiny crack in the ceiling rock, shining directly on Tom. Surrounded by the light, the young boy felt a remarkable sensation. He sucked in hard, as if attempting to take the light into his lungs and carry it throughout his body.

"Do you love me, Jesus?" Tears streaked down Tom's face.

The light was gone as the sun continued its rotation, and Tom shivered in sudden coldness. "Do you love me, Jesus?" It was not really a question as much as a hopeless plea.

Tom left the cave and spent three hours digging up the biggest rocks he could carry. He tightly filled the entrance to the secret place—the place where the bones of Big Earl and Poke would remain forever. The place where he sought Jesus and for a moment stood in the light. The place where one sixteen-year-old boy left what little hope remained.

The Letter: August 10

||||||||||||||||||||||||||||||||||||||||||||||||||||||||||||||||||||

You know, Tina, I really believe this writing down my life is help-ing me a great deal. I really can't express it, but just going back in my memory, although painful, seems to bring closure to so many of my tortured memories. Maybe recognizing guilt and admitting what you've done is salvation.

I also think I've learned the most important lesson of my life. I didn't know that the one thing we must have in life, if we are ever to realize and experience hope, is faith. I can't say I have it now, but at least I understand what it is. So the lesson must be: if you have faith, there is hope.

I stopped reading my Bible last night just after midnight. As I shut my eyes, my memory came back clear as a summer sky. Do you remember the day you gave me the gold ring? I've always kept it on a chain around my neck, close to my heart. The prison guards would not let me wear the chain, but I still have the ring. I was holding it in my hand the day you visited.

I'd like to recall that day with you once again. It was the last time I would see you before you visited here. It was also the day before I committed the fourth sin.

The Fourth Sin

|||||||||||||||||||||||||||||||||||||||||||||||||||||||||||||||||||

Thomas Lavon Tabor stood silently and motionless before what only hours earlier had been the entrance to his secret place. The rocks that now covered the entire hole did so in such a way that no one would recognize it as an opening to anything. The hole, now packed with large stones, blended into the hillside perfectly.

Tom walked north of the special place of a thousand flowers until he reached old man Craven's lake. He didn't give much thought to the reason why as he flung both the shovel and pick axe into the water. He turned from the muddy pool, listening to the bullfrogs resume their mating calls temporarily interrupted by the shovel-throwing boy. He climbed to the top of the hill, stopped, and stood between the two graves.

"Good-bye, Brown," he whispered. "You were a good old dog and didn't deserve to die like you did. But that's okay, boy. Poke paid for killin' ya."

Tom wiped his nose on the sleeve of his now dirty white shirt. "Good-bye, Baby. Please forgive me. If there is a heaven and Jesus lives there, you are with him, little girl."

Mrs. Brown was the first to see him standing atop the hill. The preacher, his wife, and their daughter stood waving from the driveway just moments earlier as Tina's boyfriend with the wealthy parents drove his new convertible down their gravel driveway.

"Brent," Mrs. Brown spoke softly. "Is that Tom standing up there on the hill?"

"I believe it is, honey," the preacher spoke quietly.

"Yes, it's Tom," Tina whispered with an anticipatory note. "I'll be back."

Tina did not wait for confirmation from her mother and father as she went from a steady pace to an all-out run across the meadows to the hill.

The young girl felt the gentle winds flow over her as they entangled with the fragrance of spring flowers in full bloom. Then Tom turned around to face her from a distance, and blackness seemed to dissipate the bright sunlight.

"Tom, is that you?" Tina shouted, knowing that it was him who stood stiffly, almost afraid to approach. Nearly out of breath, she reached the top of the hill. She didn't know whether to scream or cry.

Tom stood stoically, without motion or response. Covered with brown mud, he looked like he might have just crawled from his own grave.

"Oh, Tom, sweet Tom, what's wrong? What's happened to you?" Tina gently put her arms around him and pulled him to the tall grass. They sat silently for a long period before Tom spoke.

"I'm a horrible, worthless person, Tina Brown. Not even fit to sit next to you."

"Oh no, Tom, don't say things like that! You are the kindest, most gentle boy I've ever known." Tina began to sob.

"Oh, Tom, I've missed you so much. Please believe me. I've called your house a thousand times. I've looked for you at school every day. Thomas Tabor, I love you! Don't you know that?"

Color rushed to his cheeks. "How can you say that, Tina?" Anger filled his voice. "I'm nothing! I dress like a bum—I have no money, no fancy car like your boyfriend! Why, hell, Tina, I'm so stupid, I'm still in the ninth grade!"

"Stop, Tom. Please stop. Don't you know that I don't care about any of that! I love you, Thomas Tabor!" Tina grabbed his dirty face and kissed him. Tom did not respond.

His head turned from hers, and Tina strained to hear his words.

"Love me, Tina? You think I'd ever allow you to love me after all the terrible things I've done? You, Tina, the most perfect thing on this earth. How could I ever allow you to love me? Tina, even God doesn't love me!"

Tom stood and faced the field of flowers. "Look out there, Tina," he said, his voice quiet. "No flower there is as beautiful as you. And me, Tina, I'm like the weeds trying my best to take their water and sunlight. Trying to choke the life from their beautiful existence. No, Tina, you can never love me, no matter what."

Tina slid the tiny gold ring from her right hand that had "LOVE" deeply engraved across its face. Her parents had given it to her only yesterday for her sixteenth birthday.

"Here, Thomas Tabor." Tina spoke with strong conviction as she now slid the ring onto his pinkie finger. "Here, Thomas. Wear this, and know that as long as you wish, I will love you. I will wait for you. I will be there for you. I will never leave you."

Tom turned, as pain-driven tears openly streamed down his face.

"I can't let you, Tina——you are too good!"

Tom bolted toward the safety of the dark treeline as Tina fell to her knees, clutching her ribs in agonizing, heavy sobs.

"I-I ... I love you, Thomas Tabor!" Her voice filled the valley of wildflowers as the sun disappeared behind the building storm clouds.

Tom watched from the forest shadows as the only person he'd ever love slowly moved through the waist-high clover, weeping.

He touched the gold ring and whispered, "I will always love you, Tina Brown, and this is good-bye."

Thomas Tabor spent the night in the woods, standing in that same spot until dawn broke over the pines above the forever-secret place.

"Tom." His mother's cry sounded extremely weak this morning. He could not remember the last time Sherrell had eaten anything more than a cracker or vanilla wafer. Her skin was tightly drawn over bones that looked like they might break through at any minute, making her bleeding mouth that much more horrible to see.

"What, Mom—what is it?" Tom shivered as he looked down and for a moment thought he was seeing his sister Baby.

"I need Valiums, son." Every word was a strain. "Go see Doctor Jackson; hurry." Sherrell's eyes rolled back before she once again curled into the fetal position.

Tom returned three hours later with a full bottle of Valium 10s. The prescription read, *Take one tablet every twelve hours.*

Tom found the cutting board under the sink and pulled the tenderizing mallet from the second drawer, left of the stove. It took him nearly twenty minutes to crush the entire bottle except one solitary pill. He poured the white powder into a half glass of grape Kool-Aid, Sherrell's favorite.

Tom sat at the edge of the bed, gently running his hand over his mother's bony face. Sherrell, once a beautiful woman, now weighed sixty-seven pounds.

"Here you go, Mom; I've got your medicine. Come on, now. Be a good girl; take your pill."

Sherrell groaned in agony as she rolled over toward her son. Her lips were bloody, cracked, and parched from dehydration. Tom was forced to momentarily look away.

"Here, Mom. Here's your pill."

Sherrell struggled to swallow the white, oblong pill. She took a small sip of grape Kool-Aid, pushing the pill down her throat with great discomfort. As she took yet another sip, her eyes appeared to brighten and her expression changed dramatically. Sherrell looked at the glass quizzically and then into her son's eyes.

"Thank you, sweet boy," she whispered. "Dear God, thank you."

Sherrell, with much difficulty, lifted the glass to her bleeding lips and drained its contents. She smiled up at Tom, rolled over, and died.

"Good night, Mother," Tom said softly.

The Last Good-bye

||||||||||||||||||||||||||||||||||||||||||||||||||||||||||||||||

The county coroner ruled Sherrell Tabor's death a suicide. There would be no funeral or grieving ceremonies. At the tender age of sixteen, Thomas Tabor stood alone and filled the hole where his mother lay in a pine box supplied by the coroner's office.

He did not shed a tear that cloudy day. He wanted to feel something, anything. But hard as he tried, there were no emotions to be summoned as the warm spring rain left tiny valleys in the fresh dirt across the mound covering his dead mother.

"Good-bye, Mother. Good-bye, Baby. Good-bye, Brown. I'm leaving now." Tom spoke monotonously, without a flicker of passion.

He turned from the fresh gravesite and for the last time looked beyond the meadow to the hillside that would hide his sins. A twisted smile shaped his face in almost evil distortion.

"See ya in hell, Poke and Big Earl!" Tom walked from the gravesite without looking back.

It didn't take him long to pack the few things he owned in the duffle bag once belonging to Big Earl. For a moment, he thought it might be nice if he could take some mementos of his family, maybe like a picture. He could not ever remember having a photo made, and his quick search only produced a shot of Sherrell and Big Earl sitting at a table in front of a smoldering ashtray surrounded by numerous empty beer bottles. He tossed the picture to the floor.

As he cleaned out the two wardrobe drawers containing all his clothing, he found the tiny New Testament with the small black-and-white photo of himself, Tina, and the big yellow dog, the only picture of his childhood, which Tina's dad had taken after his first Sunday dinner with the Brown family. He gently placed the Bible and picture inside the duffle bag.

Tom took one last look around before leaving the Tabor shack forever. He could not say why, but he felt drawn to the nightstand by his mother's bed. He sat on the bed for several minutes just looking at the nightstand, almost afraid to open it.

The top drawer he found to be full of worthless junk, empty medicine bottles, and several *Movie Screen* magazines. In the bottom drawer, Tom found a solitary metal box.

Carefully opening the box, he jumped quickly to his feet in total shock. The green metal container was stuffed with ten- and twenty-dollar bills. Once counted, Thomas Tabor crammed $1,960 in his front pants pocket. At the bottom of the box lay a sealed envelope simply marked, TOM. With a great deal of trepidation, the boy opened the envelope.

Dear Tom:

I know I ain't been much of a mother, and I can't say I have any excuses. Life's been tough on all my children, and I guess I am mostly to blame for that. Even though I ain't been all that good, I do love my kids, and, Tom, you have been my special one.

Since I brung you into this cold, old world, your daddy has sent me money for you from time to time. I have saved every dollar to give you someday, for a new start.

I've not seen or heard from your father for a long time. I know he is an officer in the marines, and last I heard, your daddy was stationed in Camp Pendleton, California. Maybe he is still there. I just can't say for sure.

Tom, your daddy's name is Josh Wildman. I love you, Tom.
Mother

Tom carefully folded the letter, placing it inside his nylon jacket pocket.

"Josh Wildman," he whispered. "My father."

As dusk came upon the Tabor shack and the darkness seemed to once again deliver the ever-present sense of evil, Tom exited the house via the back door.

Striking the kitchen match against his blue jeans, Tom watched the yellow-blue flame as if it held a special magic— a simple flicker of flame that might burn from his memory the tortures of his youth. The fire that could engulf his sins and burn them into oblivion. Tom tossed the match upon the kitchen floor. The filth and grease that covered the rotten wood ignited with fury.

Tom felt the heat as the blaze erupted. He unconsciously rubbed his hands, stretching his arms out to the glorious warmth of the glowing fire.

"Good-bye … and good riddance."

No one saw the figure of the boy walk from the burning shack as the fire cast his shadow before him.

"I have a father."

Tom walked throughout the night, attempting to decide what his next move might be. He stopped at the diner for breakfast while waiting for *Ernie's Like New Used Cars* to open.

Tom purchased a 1962, green Volkswagen bus, figuring he could also live in the vehicle as he made his way west.

"Hey, Ernie."

"Yeah, son?"

"Do you know how to get to the West Coast?"

"Geez-o-pete, boy, I ain't sure how to find Kentucky!" The fat man with a pencil-thin mustache shook like Jell-O as he laughed long and loud. "But, hey, I got one of them there atlases that got every map of all forty states. Let's have a look and see."

"Tell you what, Ernie, how 'bout I give you five bucks for the map book?"

"Well, I'd say you gots yourself a fine automobile and a whole lot of maps to take her drivin' through, boy!"

"By the way, son, where you headed?" Ernie stuck a fat cigar in between his yellowish teeth.

"California, Ernie. I'm going to see my dad." Tom waved good-bye as the green Volkswagen headed west.

The Letter: August 11

IIIIIIIIIIIIIIIIIIIIIIIIIIIIIIIIIIIIIIIIIIIIIIIIIIIIIIIIIIIIIIIIIIII

After Mom was buried and I'd said goodbye to you the previous Sunday, I knew there wasn't much left to keep me in Ironton, Ohio.

As I drove west, my thoughts remained focused on you. I would touch the ring you gave me and recall every word you spoke at the special place. To this day, I remember the softness of your lips when you kissed me. The fragrance of your hair and the beauty of your slender fingers are memories that linger as if it were only yesterday.

So many times my heart pleaded with me to turn around. Your final words—"I love you, Thomas Tabor"—brought me hope and yet great agony.

I thought about returning, finding a job, and going back to school. I could work hard, save my money, and maybe someday prove worthy of your love. Then the voice that never lets me sleep whispered, "Yeah, Tom, go on back. Tell your little girlfriend

where Poke and Big Earl are rotting. I'm sure she'll think you are a wonderful human being for smothering your baby sister. And oh, shucks, Tommy Boy, lots of people kill their mammas! Yeah, Tom, go on back and see how Tina's parents like their daughter loving a mass murderer!"

The evil voice that talked to me that day won the argument, as it has every day since.

Knowing I would rather die than hurt you gave me every reason to run as fast as possible. Maybe in time, I thought, the memories of my horror would pass and I could return to you.

I know this must sound absurd, but all my life I've been lying to myself, saying, "Maybe someday I'll return and find my precious Tina waiting." Pretty sad, huh?

And in the end, you were the one to return and find me on death row, prepared to pay the final price for all my sins.

As I continued my journey west in search of my father, I began to develop scenarios where I might return a different man. Yes, I could become a marine like my dad. Maybe go to war and become a hero, there would be a big parade in Ironton, and you could ride beside me in my new yellow convertible. The best laid plans of mice and men, I guess.

No matter what I dreamed or planned, it has always been devoured by the evil that overtook me as a child. No, Tina, I wouldn't come back as a hero. I was on the way to my fifth sin.

The Fifth Sin

||||||||||||||||||||||||||||||||||||||||||||||||||||||||||||||||||||||

Thomas Tabor took his sweet time driving across America. So much to think about, to worry about, to forget about.

What if my father hates me? What if he denies I'm his son? What if he tells me to go straight to hell?

Tom laughed cynically. "Sorry, Pop! Can't go straight to hell, Dad! You know why, Father? Because I just came from hell!"

Tom drove to the marine base five days in a row. Fearing rejection that might be too painful to recover from, he couldn't find the nerve to enter the front gates.

What the heck? he thought the morning of the sixth day. *Who gives a damn if he don't want to see me? I'll just tell him to kiss my butt and move on down the road!* Tom walked into the building where the red sign proclaimed "Base Reception."

"Can I help you, sir?" Tom thought it odd that the young marine with two stripes on his sleeve would call him sir.

"Uh, yes, maybe. Uh, I mean, I hope so."

The marine's expression did not change. It wasn't hard or mean looking. *Kind of businesslike,* Tom thought.

"Well, I'm, looking for my father, sir. My name is Thomas Tabor." Tom now wondered why he was calling this marine not much older than himself sir.

"I see," the marine replied. "Is your father stationed here?"

"Last I heard he was."

"Name and rank?" The marine moved to the computer screen, placing his hands upon the keyboard.

"His name is Josh Wildman, and I ain't sure of his rank at the moment. You see, I've never seen my daddy before. It's, well, how do I—"

The marine entered the name Tom had given him. He slowly looked up, and Tom could see a sudden sadness in his eyes. "If you don't mind, Mr. Tabor, please have a seat over by the drinking fountain. Somebody will be here shortly to help you."

"Thanks." Tom strangely felt a kinship with the young marine and envisioned looking like he did someday. He would make his father and Tina proud of him no matter how hard the task.

Thirty minutes passed before a large black man entered. He wore heavily starched camo fatigues with a lot of stripes on the collar of his uniform.

"Hello, son." His voice was strong yet comforting. "I'm Sergeant Major Goodin. You say Captain Wildman is your father?"

"Um, I believe so, sir." Tom's hand shook as he pulled the letter from his mother out of his back pocket, handing it to the formidable marine.

"Hmm." The sergeant major read the letter twice and handed it back to Tom. "You best come with me, son. I have something to tell you."

The sergeant major did not speak as they drove in the open-air jeep for what seemed like an eternity to Tom.

"Would you like a cup of java, son? I believe I could use a jolt of caffeine."

"Yes, sir. Thank you, sir."

The big marine smiled and left the room filled with US Marine Corps history and mementoes of triumphs long past.

Tom rose from the high-back, leather chair and walked around the office in complete awe. He reached out, touching the highly polished engraved sword with a pearl handle. He wondered what the big marine must have done to win so many medals enshrined in an enormous glass display case. And then he froze before the picture of the black man and a tall white man standing with arms around each other's shoulders in what looked like a jungle. Tom shivered, as he thought the white man looked like him, only older.

The sergeant major laced his mug of steaming coffee with a triple shot of bourbon. He knew the next several moments would be difficult.

"Know who that is, son?" the marine said softly. "That's your daddy, boy, Captain Joshua Thomas Wildman. One of the bravest men I ever had the honor of serving with."

"Is he here, sir?"

"I'm sorry to tell you this, son, but your daddy died on Charlie Ridge in the Nam. He died saving my life and the lives of ten other marines. Your daddy won the Medal of Honor, the highest medal in the military. The captain was a very brave man. He died with honor and courage, fighting for his country and his men."

Tom didn't know whether to laugh or cry.

"Yeah, well, what the heck. He didn't even know I existed."
Tom got up to leave. "Thanks for your time, sir."

"Hold on just a second, boy. There's something else I need
to tell you."

Tom slowly returned to the leather chair, not realizing he
had sat down in front of the sergeant major again.

"Your daddy knew you existed, boy; don't you ever doubt
that. I did two tours in the Nam with the captain, and he told
me all about you. You lived in Ohio, right?"

"Uh, yes, sir."

"Your mamma's name was Sheryl or Sherry—something
like that?"

"Yes, sir."

"Your daddy told me that when he got back from Vietnam
he was going to come get you and maybe teach you how to be
a marine. That's the truth boy. Your daddy knew you existed,
and he was going to bring you out here to live. But sometimes,
son, God works in ways we can't understand."

Tears welled up in Tom's eyes as he looked into the strained
face of the sergeant major.

"Yes, sir. I guess I know all about how God works in strange
ways. Yeah, I guess I know better than most."

"Tom, your daddy wasn't married, and you're his only son.
When he died, I stood in at the big ceremony in Washington
for your father. I know the captain would want you to have
this."

The sergeant reached into the top desk drawer and pulled
out a purple case. He handed it to Tom. "This belongs to you
now, son."

Tom opened the case and looked down at the Congres-
sional Medal of Honor.

"Thank you, sir. This is the greatest thing I've ever owned."

The marine pulled the white handkerchief from his pocket,
blowing his broad nose and fighting back his own tears.

"Is there anything I can do for you, son? I loved your daddy, and I'd be proud to help his boy."

"Thank you, sir, but no, I'm okay. I think I better leave now." Tom stuck out his hand to shake.

Instead of shaking the boy's hand, Sergeant Major Goodin snapped to attention and saluted. "Your daddy was a hero, Tom, and no one can ever take that away."

Tom forced a slight smile, shook his head in acknowledgment, and walked out of the office. The sergeant major followed Tom, barking orders to the young marine in the outer room.

"Corporal!"

"Yes, sir, Sergeant Major!"

"Take this fine young man to the front gate, Corporal. And best be honored to ride beside him, boy, 'cause his daddy owns the Medal of Honor!"

The young marine smiled warmly at Tom and simply stated, "Awesome!"

The young couple in bellbottom pants and tie-dye tee shirts walked along the secluded beach, sharing an expertly rolled joint of Mexican Gold.

"Oh wow, Petey, what's that over there?"

"Man, like, who knows, man? Looks like some dude all relaxed out."

"Yeah, wow, probably some stupid marine all beer-soaked up."

"Hey, Becky, watch that dude. It's like wow, he ain't moving a muscle."

The young potheads slowly approached the stretched-out body.

"Oh no, man! Holy crap! Look at the blood, Becky!"

"Run, Petey! Call the police or something."

The shore patrol was the first to arrive at the scene. A young, white male lay flat upon the beach. Both wrists had been severely slashed. Dark-red blood oozed out, disappearing into the brown sand, as the two navy men struggled to save the stranger's life.

Beside the still body, the MPs found a four-inch Hook-bill knife and stood in amazement as the flashlight glowed upon the boy's chest, with the Medal of Honor pinned above his heart.

The Letter: August 12

||||||||||||||||||||||||||||||||||||||||||||||||||||||||||||||||||||||

Over the course of the last thirty years, I've often contemplated true sin. I believe I have enough experience to be considered an expert. Killing Poke and Big Earl are probably right at the top of real sin. I'm not sure if what I did to Baby and Mamma would hit the "big sin" list. I think it was out of mercy, but I'm sure the courts, and maybe God, would look at it a bit differently.

Now, suicide is a different issue altogether. Some people that do at least attempt it like I did could probably fall into the sin category. However, if the truth be told, God might just be angry that I failed in my suicide effort. It's for sure the world would be a better place if I'd died that night on the beach.

I'm still reading my Bible each evening like you asked. There's so much to contemplate and comprehend.

Jesus has to be the kindest man that ever lived. He cared so much for people others hated. I don't know why he had to die. Just think of what it would be like to have Jesus here on earth today. I really wish I could meet him.

After I left the hospital, I mostly just hung around the streets of San Diego. I fell in with a bunch that smoked pot all day and broke into houses at night. The other guys really liked me because I wasn't afraid to do anything. They thought I was brave like my father. What a laugh, huh? Actually, it had nothing at all to do with courage. I just didn't give a damn if I lived or died.

One Sunday morning as I walked the streets in the bad part of town, stepping over the winos, I heard a familiar sound. "Jesus, Jesus, how I love him, how I love him more each day ... "

I remembered when we sang that song at your daddy's church when I couldn't have been more than seven or eight years old.

I followed the sound up to the front door of this old, shotgun building in between a pawnshop and a liquor store. Over the front door hung a small, hand-painted sign that read, GOD WORKS MISSION.

I can't say why for sure, but I felt like something pulled at me. Some unseen force pushed and tugged until I found myself inside, standing in the middle of the aisle like a moron.

Up at the front stood a man in a white robe with long black hair down to his shoulders.

"Welcome to God Works, son. Come on in and join us. Everyone is welcomed in the house of God," he had said.

Still in a daze, I eased into the closest metal chair, and for the first time since I'd gone to church with you, I felt peace.

I don't really remember much about the service except that when it ended, everyone left and I just sat there as if caught up in some unexplainable dream state.

"Hello, son; my name is Moses Aleeach. Most people in the area call me the street preacher."

I suddenly returned to reality and looked into the solid-black eyes of the man next to me. I swear I saw the sign of the cross reflecting from his dark eyes. I also felt love and warmth. To this day, I believe Jesus must have eyes just like the street preacher.

He asked me if I'd like to stay and have lunch with him and several of the God Works people. Actually, I wanted to run like hell, but something more powerful than words can explain kept my butt tight in that gray metal chair. I simply replied, "Yes, thank you."

I followed the street preacher to a back room that contained a stove, icebox, a table made of plywood on two sawhorses, and several of the same kind of metal chairs as in the main part of the building.

I was surprised to see that the five other people there were all about my age.

"Sit here next to me." The street preacher's voice sounded like what I imagine Jesus might sound like. "What's your name, son?"

"Thomas Lavon Tabor." Oh, Tina, I turned beet red and wanted to kick myself at that moment. Why, the only other time I even used my middle name was on the bus with you when I was seven years old.

"Thomas is a wonderfully strong name, son." Moses smiled and touched my shoulder.

"He's also one of the great men in the New Testament. Is it okay if I call you Thomas?"

Tina, I looked across at the spot where the high-pitched voice had come from. There before me was a skinny girl of maybe seventeen years of age, with bright orange hair the color of an autumn pumpkin. Her entire face looked like it had been splattered with tiny brown paint spots.

You know, since I left home, I had never looked at another girl. I can't say I was really looking at this one either. But I did see something special. Best way to describe it would be, I guess, like a friend holding out her hand. Know what I mean?

Moses Aleeach was the kindest man I've ever known, Tina. He trusted me like a son, and the girl with the pumpkin hair? Well, I'm pretty sure she loved me.

I guess that was the best place I ever found—full of love, hope, and giving. And how did I repay them for most likely saving my life? What did I give back in return for allowing me to become part of their family? Nothing, Tina, absolutely nothing.

Instead, after giving me their complete love and trust, I repaid them by committing my sixth sin ...

The Sixth Sin

‖‖

Tom could actually sense the strength and power of the incredible man dressed in a frayed robe that appeared to have been made by hand. The rugged, off- white garment only accentuated his long black hair and dark, gleaming eyes. When the street preacher looked at you, you could not move, as every ounce of your being longed to absorb his love.

"Well, Thomas, now that we know who you are, allow me to introduce my bank of Jesus-loving misfits!" Everyone laughed in unison.

"To your left is Steve, our recovering heroin addict. On the right you'll find Nate, the car thief. Across from you is Blair, ex-prostitute, who is sitting next to Ricky, who has been a serious alcoholic since the tender age of twelve."

"I only drink orange juice now!" Ricky joked.

"And then, in the middle, is our sweet little magpie, Clairese. But feel free to call her Red—we all do."

"Well, tell him what I've done, Moses." Clairese seemed offended for being left out of the sins of the past stories.

"Okay, Red." Moses laughed warmly. "Thomas, our sweet little Clairese has done the same things the rest of the group has done, and then a lot more. Happy now, Red?"

"Yes, Moses, very. Thank you so much for sharing our splendid backgrounds with our guest, Thomas."

"You're welcome, young lady. Now if you don't mind, let's eat!"

The vegetable soup might have had several small pieces of meat, Tom surmised, and was a bit short of recognizable vegetables. But it was hot, and he felt at peace with the God Works misfits.

Red broke off an end of the large loaf of French bread, dipping it into the greasy soup.

"Um, Red?" Moses tilted his head, looking disappointed in the process. "Don't you think we should thank the Lord before we feed our hungry faces?"

"Sorry, Moses."

"That's okay, Red. Why don't you say grace?"

"Yes, sir." The other teenagers reached out, clasping hands. Tom momentarily pulled back but enjoyed the touch of other human beings doing something so sincere.

"Dear heavenly Father," Red began. "Thank you for this wonderful meal of what I'm guessing is vegetable soup." Moses opened one eye, grinning in Red's direction. "And thank you for taking all of us off the street before it was too late. And also thank you, dear Lord, for Moses, our earthly father. Amen."

Red suddenly raised her hands, indicating that her prayer was not yet finished. "One more thing, dear Lord: thank you for bringing Thomas to us. In the name of Jesus Christ, our Lord, we pray, amen. And that's the end!" Red giggled.

Halfway through the meal of watery soup, white bread with margarine, and iced tea, Red asked in a matter-of-fact way. "So, Thomas, now you know all the bad stuff on us. What's your big, dark secret?"

Moses watched the boy carefully, ready to intervene if necessary. He also knew that confession is good for the soul, so he waited to see Tom's reaction.

Tom smiled as he looked at each of the teenagers individually, and he thought, *Boy, could I blow this group clean out of the water. Oh well, let's see here. What has Thomas Lavon Tabor done that would compare to the sins of the group? Well, how 'bout we start with four murders?* He decided to hold up on those stories.

Again smiling, Tom slowly rolled up his shirtsleeves, raised his arms, and turned from side to side so everyone could get a good look at his scars. "How does trying to kill yourself work? Will that get me in the misfits?" Tom laughed and weirdly felt proud of his suicide attempt.

"Oh, that's weak, Thomas!" Red exclaimed, which set Tom back a bit. "Heck, Thomas, we've all tried to kill ourselves!"

Moses spit tea down his robe as the room erupted in teenage laughter. Tom joined in the laughter as well, looking across into the flashing green eyes set among a million freckles. "You are something else, Red; you really are."

"Same to you, Thomas, I'm sure."

"It'll take a while, Thomas, but she'll grow on you," Moses added.

"Let's hope," Red replied, trying to use her sexy voice.

After the meal of soup and bread, Moses invited Thomas to his office. The two men walked down a dimly lit hallway where Tom could see tiny rooms on each side. The doorway to each room remained open. As Tom glanced from side to side, he assumed the small chambers were the living quarters of the misfits.

"Here we go," Moses spoke cheerfully. "My humble abode."

Tom walked into the cramped quarters and wondered if most jail cells could be as confining.

"Nice place." He attempted to sound sincere.

Moses smiled. "Yes, it is, Thomas. Real nice—that is, if you like living in a sardine can."

The room contained a small metal bed neatly made against the right wall. At the back of the room sat a wooden desk that looked like it could have been retrieved from any garbage dump. Two metal chairs completed the ensemble. Nothing covered the walls except a large wooden cross over the iron bed.

"Where do you live, Thomas?"

"Oh, I share an old house with four other guys down by Balboa Park."

"And what do you and your friends do for a living?"

Tom blushed and decided not to answer directly. For whatever reason, he didn't wish to lie to this decent man. "You know, a little of this, a little of that."

Moses smiled, and Tom knew instantly that the street preacher knew "this and that" ain't what normal people do.

"So, Moses, what's this God Works thing all about?"

"Well, Thomas, it's a very long story that might be best told at a later date. But let me give you the *Reader's Digest* version."

Moses sat down on the edge of the iron bed, and Tom pulled up a gray metal chair. "Several years ago, I came to this part of the country, not really knowing or caring why."

"I know the feeling."

"Yes." Moses paused for a moment. "My life had been filled with hate, loneliness, and far too many nights in jails across America. I've done some pretty horrific things, Thomas, and

I thank God every day for his grace and forgiveness. I arrived in San Diego flat broke. Without any skills or real desire to do an honest day's work, I went about doing what I did best— selling drugs, beating up people for money, stealing, robbing, and anything else that brought easy cash without much work involved."

Tom thought how wonderful it would be to tell the truth. Maybe someday he could.

"I'd just completed sixty days in jail for drunk and disorderly when I met a man at the Southside Soup Kitchen. This man was like no one I had ever met before. You felt real love just standing next to him."

Tom realized he felt the same thing being near the street preacher.

"Out of the clear blue sky this remarkable man gave me and others in the soup line a fifty-dollar bill and a card that read, 'God Works,' with an address on the back."

Moses paused as if in deep thought and then laughed, shaking his head. "I swear, Thomas, everyone in the soup line bolted immediately as if shot from a cannon. I watched them all move from soup kitchen to liquor store like a bunch of wild Indians."

"What did you do, Moses?" Tom asked with intense interest.

"I couldn't do anything. It was as if I became frozen in place. I looked around, seeing all the small, white God Works cards upon the dirty sidewalk that the other men had discarded in eager search of today's bottle of port. I turned and watched the man who left me speechless walk down the street, and I honestly believe I saw an aura of light illuminate from his body."

"Who was this guy, Moses?"

"His name is Uriah Mann, and he is the godliest person I have ever known."

"Was he a street preacher too?"

"In a way, but much bigger, better, and more giving than I will ever be."

"Did you ever see him again?"

"Yes, Thomas, I did. Several days passed before I worked up the courage to visit the address on the God Works card. From the time I received the card until I entered the mission, I did not eat anything, drink any alcohol, do any drugs, and hardly slept. I just knew I could not go on until I talked to the man of light."

"Wow, this guy sounds like an angel or something."

Moses laughed. "Who's to say? If there is one thing I learned in life it is this: God can, will, and does unbelievable things that cannot be explained. There's a miracle waiting every moment. You just have to have faith and continue to search for God's will."

"So did you meet this, uh, Uriah Mann fella?"

"Yes." Tom watched in amazement as the street preacher's eyes seemed to glow. For an instant, he believed he might also be seeing the aura surround Moses.

"I walked into the building on a Saturday night nearly two years ago. Standing in the doorway, afraid to move any farther, I watched Uriah sweep the floor. He was quietly singing 'Amazing Grace.'"

"Pretty far out, huh?"

"Oh, it gets better, Thomas, much better."

Tom leaned forward, enthralled in the story.

"Uriah slowly turned, leaned against the broom, and smiled in a way that it seemed the whole room filled with love.

"'Moses,' Uriah said, Thomas, and I nearly passed out. 'I've been waiting for you.' I wondered how he knew my name."

"Did he ever tell you?"

"Yes. He said God told him who I was."

"Unbelievable," Tom whispered.

"Anyway, Uriah put the broom down and reached out his hand toward me. 'Come, Moses. Come kneel and pray with me. Jesus has called you.' I couldn't stop my motion. I stumbled, fell to the floor, and crawled like a child until I lay at the feet of Uriah Mann. 'Jesus loves you, Moses, and wishes to forgive your sins. Let Jesus into your heart, my friend. God has a plan for you, and today is the new beginning.' I wept so hard that my entire body ached. There on that floor, Thomas, with Uriah kneeling beside me, the spirit of God ran though me like a bolt of lightning. When we finished praying, I knew my sins were forgiven and I would do whatever God directed."

"So what happened to Uriah?"

"Shortly after my conversion, Uriah told me how God Works had established missions for people without hope all across the country."

"Are they all like this one?"

"Pretty much, as I understand it."

"Do you and the others here have to work to pay rent and buy the things that you need?"

"No, son. Uriah's instructions were clear. Our mission is to help the lost find God and reclaim their souls. That's a full-time job, believe me."

"So how do you get money?"

"That in itself is a miracle. Every month, like clockwork, I receive a personal check from Uriah Mann. It is never the same amount, but always the exact amount we need to get us through a new month."

"How long do people stay here?"

"As long as they need to. So far, I have worked with twenty-seven young adults on their journey to recovery and salvation."

"Where do they go—you know, when they're fixed?" Tom wished that question could be asked a bit more diplomatically.

"Oh, some get married, three have started a new mission up north, and several are attending college."

"Did any ever go back to the street?"

"No, Thomas, thank the Lord. Once you truly find Jesus, it's almost impossible to turn away."

"Jesus," Tom spoke softly.

"Yes, Jesus. Have you ever thought about Jesus?"

Tom recalled the cave at that moment and the stone wall with the carving of Jesus. He remembered standing in the light, and then he remembered Poke and Big Earl.

"Well, Moses, I really have to be going now." Tom wanted to run, not really knowing why.

"I understand, Thomas. Please come back to see us."

"Yes, I will." Tom felt nervous. "Thanks for the lunch."

"You're welcome, son."

Several weeks passed as Tom continued to fight the inner turmoil supplied by one longhaired, crazy street preacher. After leaving the mission, he returned to the rundown dwelling to find all his buddies in crime sprawled out in every direction, either in a drunken stupor or sky high on coke. He left and began living in the Volkswagen bus once again.

Tom sat before the fire on a secluded section of beach up the way from Balboa Park. Two empty Ripple bottles lay at his feet as he gulped down a huge swallow of the third bottle of cheap red wine. He began to cry.

"Jesus? Are you here, Jesus? Can you see me, Jesus? Do you love me, Jesus?"

Drained of all emotion and two steps ahead of drunk, Tom pulled his knees to his chest and rested his head upon his arms. He contemplated suicide once again.

Tom nearly wet his pants when the tiny, high-pitched voice shot out of the blackness.

"Hey, Thomas Lavon Tabor, that's a lot of wine for just one person."

Tom turned his head quickly to find a thousand freckles surrounding a very white smile.

"What are you doing here?" His voice was filled with surprise.

"Better yet, Thomas, what are you doing here?"

"Getting drunk! What's it look like, Red?"

"Your description is adequate, I'd say."

"And what the hell you doing out here by yourself, girl?"

"Looking for you." Clairese spoke matter-of-factly.

"Huh?" Tom struggled to stand.

"Steve left yesterday to join the navy, which means we have a vacant slot open now in the misfits."

"Yeah, okay, so? How the hell did you find me, anyway?"

"Moses told me where to find you. It's weird, I know, but he does stuff like that all the time."

"Then how the hell did he know where the hell I was?"

"Probably didn't, Thomas. I'd guess God told him where you were. Now come on; it's getting cold out here."

Red held out her slender hand. Tom in turn clasped his sand-covered hand around hers and allowed the frail teenager to lead him off into the night. It was as if Red guided a ghost into the darkness. Tom couldn't say why he followed, nor did he care. All Tom knew for sure was that he was at least walking away from nothing, and that provided enough reason to move.

Tom enjoyed living at the mission and worked hard keeping the place clean. He painted the outside and inside of the building. It took almost a month for him to sand the chapel floor and re-varnish the wood. He stayed busy, always eager to do whatever, but Tom did not really feel part of the group. He didn't know how to belong.

After six months in the mission, Moses came into Tom's room late one evening.

"Well, Thomas, you've been with us now nearly six months. I want to thank you for all you've done around here. It's for sure hard work doesn't scare you."

"Ah heck, Moses, it's the least I can do. You've fed me, gave me a place to live, bought me clothes—I only wish I could do more."

Moses smiled. "Thomas, do you want to know Jesus?"

Tom lowered his head, giving serious thought to the street preacher's question, secretly worrying that something was terribly wrong within himself. The other people at the mission seemed so happy and sure of God's love. He, on the other hand, woke each morning recalling the previous night's dreams of his past atrocities.

"Yes, Moses, I would." Tom hesitated. "But I can't."

"And why is that, son?"

"I'm not good enough to be loved by anyone, especially the Son of God."

"There's a whole lot of people in the Bible that I'm sure did worse things than you, Thomas, and Jesus loved them the most!"

Tears began to slowly run down Tom's flushed cheeks. "Worse things, Moses? Worse than murder? Worse than killing your brother, sister, and mother? Worse things? I don't think so, Moses, I really don't."

It would be one of the few times Moses could recall being speechless.

"Thomas, by the blood of Jesus, God forgives all sin. Yes, even murder. Would you like to tell me about it?"

Tom looked the street preacher right in the eyes, wanting desperately to unload his awesome burden of guilt. Then the inner voice took control.

Are you crazy, Thomas Tabor? You don't know this rag picker that likes to act like he's holy. Wise up, boy! He could run to the cops if you spill your guts. Would you like to take the last ride in the electric chair?

"No, Moses, not tonight. I'm just not ready to talk about the past."

"I understand, Thomas. Can I pray with you?"

"Sure."

Moses prayed from his very soul. He pleaded with God to heal the scars of this young man's spirit. Tom did not hear a single word of the street preacher's prayers. The inner voice kept him from listening.

Tom lay in bed that night fighting the evil presence that had almost disappeared for a time. Now it came back, grasping him so tightly that breathing became difficult.

Get the hell away from these whackos, Tom. Moses is a freak and a fake. He'll tell the cops on you, Tommy Boy, and then you'll get to go to your own barbeque. Run, Thomas Tabor, the evil voice seemed to hiss. *Run.*

At three a.m., Tom quietly walked into Red's room. He pulled her covers back, sliding his body up next to hers. Clairese stiffened as Tom cupped his hand over her tiny breast.

"What are you doing, Thomas?" Her voice bordered on rage.

"You're special, Red. I think I love you. Please make love to me tonight. In the morning, we'll run away together. We'll go to Mexico!"

Red turned suddenly and with surprising power, caused Tom to fall upon the floor.

"Mexico? Are you nuts or something?"

The click of the light switch sounded like a bomb went off to Tom. The room exploded in yellow light. Tom had no place to run or hide and felt like a complete and total fool, sitting on the floor wearing only his boxer shorts.

Red shook her head sadly. "I don't know what's wrong with him, Moses. I think the boy needs help!"

As hard as it might have been for Tom to concede, this had to be the absolute most humiliating moment in his life.

Tom could not look at the strained, painful expression upon the face of the man who had given him trust, understanding, and yes, love.

"We can't have this, Thomas. I'm afraid you must leave."

Tom stood, not looking at Moses or Red, and walked to his room. Five minutes later, he opened the front door of the mission, peering out into the darkest night in his memory.

"Thomas." Moses stood before the simple altar made of two-by-fours. "Come back, son, when you're ready to shed the burdens and reach out for God's love."

Tom once again saw the gleam in the street preacher's eyes, turned back to the darkness, and walked away into the night.

Moses Aleeach remained on his knees, praying for the boy until daylight.

Red ran into the mission early the following afternoon, holding the only envelope the postman delivered that day. Moses opened it and whispered, "Praise God." The envelope contained a check for two thousand dollars, endorsed by Uriah Mann.

"Whew." Red blew out her breath in relief. "And just in the nick of time. Amen!"

Moses also expressed a flood of relief. The rent and utilities were due, Nate's dental bill amounted to four hundred dollars, and the cupboard now contained a can of tuna, half a box of crackers, and a ninety-nine cent bag of puffed wheat cereal.

He signed the check and instructed Red to hurry down to the bank to cash it before closing time.

Moses turned the key, locking the front door of the mission at half past six. He and the band of misfits were off to their Wednesday-night prayer meeting services at the section of beach where the teenage druggies hung out. Tom watched from the alleyway across from the God Works mission as the Christian group departed.

At dark, Tom slipped over the rickety back fence and pulled the key from under the concrete angel that guarded the rear entrance to the mission.

It wasn't a secret where Moses kept the money for the mission. Tom reached under the street preacher's bed, collecting the shoebox.

"Holy moly," Tom whispered as he counted twenty, one hundred-dollar bills. "Guess you'll have to give old Uriah a call first thing in the morning!"

Tom folded the cash, stuffing it greedily into his pants pocket.

Heavy guilt persisted as Thomas Tabor drove east, trying to get as far away as possible from God Works and the street preacher. He could now add stealing from Christian people to his ever-growing list of sins.

The Letter: August 13

|||||||||||||||||||||||||||||||||||||||||||||||||||||||||||||||||||||

Well, just seventeen more days to payback time! You know what is really spooky, Tina? I have just a little over two weeks to live, and I'm not the least bit scared. Probably just too stupid to be afraid, or more likely, just too tired of living to care anymore.

I finished reading Revelation last night. Man, now that's some serious reading. If all those things are really going to happen anytime soon, then maybe I'm the lucky one! You know, get the heck out of dodge before all hell breaks loose!

I have really enjoyed the Bible you gave me. It is so hard to imagine what it would be like to actually meet Jesus. Now, that thought really does frighten me. Can't you just see it?

"Oh, hi, Jesus. Thanks a lot for getting beat like a dog, tortured, and nailed to a cross. Man, that was really a cool thing for you to *do, and just for me. And because you suffered like no man should, I just get to waltz right on into heaven and live happily ever after!"*

Nah, Tina, I just can't believe that's the way it works. All my life, I've committed the most horrific of sins—unspeakable atrocities without remorse. And now, just as I'm about to pay the price for all the evil I've done, Jesus forgives me? I can't find any justice in that, Tina, and Christ paid far too high a price to allow forgiveness for a wretch like me.

Don't get me wrong, now. I do believe in Jesus as the Son of God. I have no doubt that heaven and hell exist. But could God forgive someone like me? Could I actually walk around heaven with people like Peter and Paul? Would it be fair to be among people like you that earned the right to be with Jesus? Oh, Tina, I know deep within my heart that I would not be able to even look upon the feet of Jesus.

You see, being executed in seventeen days is not a punishment to me. Sadly enough, I'm really kind of looking forward to it. I've truly been an evil man, and now it's time to pay the piper. My punishment must be equal to my sins. An eternity in hell with other evil souls I believe to be adequate justice, and I'm now ready to pay that price.

Enough about hell, huh? I'll be there before you know it.

After I robbed Moses, the guilt became almost overwhelming. All I could think about was getting as far away as possible from the street preacher. Without much thought, I just kept driving until I'd reached Ironton once again.

I can't really say why I came back. Most likely it was in hopes of seeing you one last time. Deep down, I knew we'd never talk or touch again. I could not allow my evilness to get close to you. But that didn't take away my hunger to just get a passing glimpse of the only person I had ever loved.

The morning I arrived back in Ironton, I bought a local newspaper and stopped for coffee at the diner. It was there I read your wedding announcement: "Tina Maria Brown to wed Michael

Klansky at 2:00 p.m." The article went on to explain how you both would be attending law school in the fall.

Tina, I ran from the diner like a crazy person and began to throw up right in the middle of the sidewalk, with people all around. I heaved my guts out for so long that I actually fell to my knees and literally crawled like a street wino to my car.

I could hear people talking: "Ain't that Tommy Tabor?"

"He always was a loser."

"Remember his mother?"

"Yeah, wasn't she the town whore?"

"The whole family was nothing but white trash."

I truly wanted to explode at that moment.

Tina, you never knew that I stood shaking like a naked man standing in a frigid storm when you walked out of church that day.

I trembled so violently that I was forced to wrap my arms around the maple tree where I hid and watched my only love leave the little church as a married woman. That day was the last time I really wept.

For the next few years I traveled all across the country, working odd jobs and mostly staying drunk. I can't even recall all the places I drifted to during that period of my life.

I eventually ended up in Wichita, Kansas, where I met a single, divorced mom with a beautiful young daughter. Did I fall in love? I'm not really sure I'm capable of such a thing. But I did desperately care for Ellen and her little girl, Pammy.

It really didn't matter what I felt, however. Satan still owned me and would never let me go. It was then and there that his evil presence stood firmly beside me as I committed the seventh sin.

The Second Chance

||||||||||||||||||||||||||||||||||||||||||||||||||||||||||||

Tom walked from his one-room existence at the Blue Star Motel for nearly a mile, until he reached the restaurant. The routine had not changed for the past six weeks.

He would awake early, usually around 5:30 a.m., when the truckers would start their big diesels. Before lighting his first Pall Mall, he would pee and then puke for several minutes. Most of the time, all he could heave was a mixture of bile and blood. Following the final few minutes of dry heaving, Tom would stand in the hot shower, bent over, as he held tightly to his burning stomach alive with red-hot ulcers.

The first shot of cheap whiskey always fought its way back up his throat as his stomach churned in retaliation. Then the second shot took hold, and the third began to make its soothing way to his brain.

It was always the same. Pee, throw up, shower, put down three shots, step into his faded jeans, and open the door to Room 13 at the Blue Star Motel, "Truckers Welcome."

The smell of burnt diesel permeated the morning air as Tom stood bare-chested in the doorway, watching the prostitutes crawl out of the big-rig tractors.

"Another day, another dollar." Tom spoke to no one, considering how much this environment might actually parallel hell itself.

Returning to the small motel room he shared with numerous cockroaches, Tom turned the black and white television to the cartoon channel. He laughed, realizing that his only joy of the day would come from Fred Flintstone and Barney Rubble.

"Morning boys." Tom smirked. "Here's to ya!" He pulled hard at the pint of whiskey for his fourth shot of the new day. "Yabba dabba doo!"

After fighting off a brief ulcer attack, he laced his K-Mart tennis shoes and slipped into his cleanest white tee shirt.

"Looking mighty sharp today, Tommy Boy," he told himself with great cynicism. "Bet there's an executive position just waiting for you to apply for." He began to sing "Working at the Car Wash Blues."

After *The Flintstones,* Tom walked along the country road, fighting the backlash of frequent eighteen-wheelers until he reached the Waffle House. He hoped Ellen would be there this morning.

"Hey, Tom!" Ellen spoke cheerfully as she worked the counter, the grill, the dirty dishes, and everything in between.

"Hey, Ellen," Tom responded. "Where's Dougie this morning?"

"It's Monday, Tom," Ellen said matter-of-factly. "Dougie is most likely still drunk from the weekend. Either that, or in jail."

Tom laughed as he wondered what really might have happened to the old black man who was a hell of a cook, just not real dependable.

"Same as always, Tom?"

"Yeah, Ellen, coffee and toast. Thanks."

Tom walked over to the booths that faced the gravel parking lot and picked up the discarded morning paper, flipping through to the want ads.

He immediately skipped over the bigger ads, knowing full well his meager experience would not be nearly adequate.

Tom sipped his hot black coffee, mulling over his true qualifications.

Let's see now, he thought. *What kind of job ad am I looking for?*

Murderer Wanted: Must be able to kill without remorse. Applicant should be experienced in hiding dead bodies and have the ability to disappear quickly.

Or maybe I could find a job like, Robber Wanted: Can you steal from innocent church people? Do you have a strong background in robbing from the poor? If you do, call 1–800-CROOK!

"Hey, Tom!" Ellen shouted as she furiously attempted to do the job of two people. "Come get your toast."

Tom walked to the pink Formica counter to fetch his meager breakfast. The plate contained his ordered toast, four scrambled eggs, bacon, and grits.

"Uh, excuse me, Ellen, I only ordered toast, and—"

"Shoosh now, Tom, can't you see I'm busy. Guess the cook made a mistake. Now you'll have to eat it!" Ellen's smile felt warm to Tom.

"Thanks," Tom whispered and returned to the want ads.

"Route Driver Wanted," Tom read. "Guess not, since I lost my license after my third DUI."

"Lawn Care Worker." Tom circled the number with his blue Bic pen and decided he'd call later that day.

With $132.85 to his name, Tom knew he'd better find a job real soon or face the option of soup kitchen line standee.

Since robbing Moses at the God Works Mission, Tom swore off stealing as a means of support, one of the few things he did right in his life.

He tried on numerous occasions to save the money he'd stolen from Moses. Tom needed to pay it back with interest. Explaining that desire was difficult, but the only people Tom loved in his entire life remained Tina and the godly man he ripped off.

"Shit," he whispered, hating himself for being such a lowlife.

Tom glanced up from the futile want-ad adventure as Levi Weinstein pulled into the lot in his gold Cadillac with the personalized license plate that read "MONEY."

Mr. Weinstein owned the Waffle House, the convenience store across the street, and the drive-thru liquor store where Tom would be in an hour or so.

Weinstein pushed through the door as if he might be royalty. And in this godforsaken part of Kansas, he was damn near close to it.

Tom chuckled as he surveyed the short Jewish man's appearance. His five-foot height was made several inches taller by what looked like patent-leather Beatle boots. His white, curly hair dyed black was near the gloss of shoe polish. His bell-bottom polyester pants were the color of Tidy Bowl with a yellow, silk shirt unbuttoned almost to his navel so his thick chest hair stuck out like a groomed poodle. Tom could not be sure but guessed there to be at least fifteen gold chains around Levi's fat neck. Of course, Weinstein wore a pinkie ring on each hand, accentuated by the enormous fake Rolex and a two-inch wide gold bracelet.

"Man, does this old guy even know what a clown he is?" Tom snickered.

"Darling!" Levi bellowed as he opened his arms in recognition of Ellen. "My poor baby, you work too hard! Uncle Levi just might have to consider giving you a big, fat raise!"

"Not in this lifetime," Ellen responded without turning to face the owner/clown.

"Now, now, my pretty little waitress, how 'bout if Uncle Levi tells you that you're going to be the manager? Huh? How 'bout that? Cat got your tongue, beautiful?"

Ellen turned, wiped her face with the moist counter towel, and smiled. "Okay then, Uncle Levi, what's the manager's job pay?"

"Darling!" Levi acted hurt. "Money? Is that all my employees think of? We're talking opportunity, sweetie! The chance of a lifetime!"

Tom had turned sideways in his booth to watch this comedy unfold.

"I'll tell you what, Weinstein, you can take this job and stick it where the sun don't shine!"

Tom smiled, admiring the courage displayed by this petite young woman.

"Ellen!" Levi shrieked. "I'm stunned! Must you attack the man who pays you with vulgarity?"

"Go to hell, Levi. I'm outta here." Ellen threw her bib apron on the counter. Weinstein unconsciously picked up the greasy apron and wiped the sweat from his furrowed brow.

"Twenty-five dollars more a week!" his voice erupted.

"Make it fifty!" Ellen shot back, standing tall with her hands firmly on her shapely hips.

"Forty!"

Ellen smiled and threw a wet dishtowel at Weinstein. "Deal, you tight little Jew. But I want a new cook hired today!"

"I will try, sweetheart, but it will take time. You must understand."

Tom rose and walked toward the pleading little man.

"Excuse me, sir, but I couldn't help but hear your conversation, and well, I'm looking for work."

Weinstein turned, cocking his right eye as if inspecting a large diamond. "I see, mister … ?"

"Tom, sir. Thomas Tabor."

"Can you cook, boy?"

"Yes, sir, I'm an excellent cook." Tom, of course, was lying through his teeth. He could fry Spam and maybe scramble an egg. But culinary expertise was not on his past list of accomplishments.

"Good!" Levi beamed as he resolved this day's business crisis. "You can start tomorrow at $4.50 an hour."

"Make it five dollars!" Ellen stated firmly. "And he starts right now!"

"Money, money, money! Is that all you think about, my child?"

"You're the teacher." Ellen smiled, showing her beautiful white teeth surrounded by full lips.

"Okay, okay, five dollars an hour. Now let me leave before I go broke."

Weinstein hurried for the door.

"Levi," Ellen spoke in a low, sexy voice. "Thank you. We love you, sweet little guy." Ellen and Tom both laughed.

Weinstein waved a hand in annoyance. "But will you love me when I'm in the poor house? Money, money, money," he cried as if dying.

"Okay then, Tom, welcome aboard! Can you really cook?"

Tom knew he could not lie his way out. "Nope, not a lick."

Ellen laughed. "Well, you can start by washing the dishes; I'll teach you the rest."

"Thanks, Ellen. I really did need a job."

Ellen turned to face him, and for an instant, their eyes met. Both blushed and turned away.

Ellen

||||||||||||||||||||||||||||||||||||||||||||||||||||||||||||||||||

Ellen Louise Pearson was born on Christmas Day, 1955. Her mother died bringing her last child into the world. Although her father attempted to hide his true feelings, Ellen knew he did not love her. Harold Pearson blamed his daughter for the death of her mother. The Pearson family consisted of two brothers, who helped their father run the seven-hundred-acre Kansas farm, and an older sister who looked more like a man than most of the boys in this rural farming community.

As Ellen grew, her older sister assumed the role of matriarch, delegating all the worst and toughest chores to her youngest sibling. Both brothers were considerably older than Ellen and simply ignored the child, as did her father.

To say Ellen's childhood was a lonely existence would be a profound understatement. Her days were filled with back-breaking work, total solitude, and void of the necessary love a child needs to blossom.

Ellen dropped out of school at the age of thirteen, not because she wasn't smart, but because her father would not buy the books and clothes she needed. Shortly after turning seventeen, her father was killed when his tractor flipped in a ravine, crushing him underneath.

Harold Pearson left three hundred acres each to his sons and one hundred acres, including the farmhouse, to the oldest daughter. He left nothing in his last will and testament for Ellen.

You could say the young girl was literally driven from her sister's house, who now lived with another ugly woman in what Ellen felt sure was an unholy relationship.

Ellen Pearson moved into a boarding house owned by whom most people called "the Wichita Witch," Miss Purdy Whiteside. To pay for her meager one room and meals, the old maid, Miss Purdy worked the seventeen-year-old girl like a mule. Ellen soon found a job as a part-time night clerk working for Levi Weinstein's quick stop convenience store at minimum wage.

She would rise at five a.m. each day, cook, clean, do the lawn care, and everything in between for the domineering Miss Witch. At six p.m., Ellen worked at Weinstein's store until midnight closing. It was there that she met Hector Rodriguez.

Hector first entered the store late one Friday evening as the radio blared warnings of a large potential tornado, an event that all in Kansas took with a grain of salt. Even so, Ellen could not help but be frightened as the night grew dark purple and the air so still that she searched for breath. Then Hector appeared.

"Good evening," the young store clerk greeted the dark Spanish man as he entered the store.

"Good evening to you, beautiful!" Hector spoke with just a trace of a Mexican accent. "Are you ready to be blown away?" His smile sparkled in the background of his brown skin and dark night.

"Just another tropical summer Kansas night." She returned his smile. "What's a tornado going to do, anyhow? Take me to Oz? I wish!"

Hector walked to the back of the store where the beer coolers were. He watched the young girl from behind the Frito-Lay rack as she stood peering out into the forbidding night. "Man, this chick is one hot momma," Hector whispered, as he truly appreciated her unique beauty.

Ellen stood just under five feet ten inches tall, weighing one hundred and ten pounds of solid muscle. Her hair, naturally curly, hung in golden ringlets to her waist. The color of liquid honey seemed to bring out the green-blue sparkle of her large eyes set wide below thick, almost black, eyebrows. In New York, she might have been a model. In Wichita, Kansas, she was only the night clerk at the convenience store.

Hector wore leather pants, the kind Ellen saw frequently worn by the numerous bikers in the area that always hit on her when they came in to buy the big quart bottles of Colt 45 Malt. His upper body displayed hard muscles inside the tight black tee shirt screen-printed with a large picture of the Zigzag man across the back.

Ellen turned from the front door and caught Hector looking at her intently. For a moment, she felt frightened, until he smiled that killer smile of his.

"Nice car," Ellen said, looking out to the gas pump where his 396 Chevy Super Sport sat.

"Yeah." Hector put his finger to his lips as if pulling out a kiss. "She's a hot, sweet little thing. Sleek, fast, classy, and mucho sexy! Kinda like you!"

Ellen blushed. "Yeah, right. I bet she cost a lot."

Now Hector laughed, giving up his sexy smile once again. "Nah, not too much. I did all the bodywork and built the engine. All the accessories I borrowed."

"Borrowed?" Ellen didn't understand.

"You know, baby, borrowed. Like found stuff just lying around. Um, like, five-finger discount!"

"Stolen?"

"Hey, baby doll, does Hector Rodriguez look like a thief to you?"

"I guess not." Ellen laughed nervously.

Hector walked to the counter with a six-pack of Bud. "So give me a pack of Marlboros, ten bucks on gas, and yeah, I need a pack of Zigzag papers."

Ellen rang his purchases and watched as the young man pulled a large wad of money from his tight pants pocket.

"Wow, that's a lot of money!"

"Ah, this ain't nothing, baby—just a little hanging-out change."

"You must have a great job. What do you do?"

"Uh, let's just say I'm in the auto transport business, international."

"Pretty impressive." Ellen was still extremely naïve.

Neither had been listening to the urgent warnings coming forth from the National Weather Service across the store's Muzak System.

Without a second's warning, the windows exploded and Ellen was flung halfway across the store.

The tornado roared like a thousand freight trains as the entire contents of the quick stop flew through the air as if they now had a life of their own. Something hard and metallic hit Ellen above the right eye, causing her to lose consciousness. Hector found himself lying in the middle of the bread rack without a scratch.

As quickly as the tornado hit, it passed. Hector heard the beautiful, young girl moaning somewhere off to his right in the darkness.

Hector's night vision was better than most, due in great part to his vocation as a world-class, late-night car thief. He crawled toward the counter and remembered seeing a display there with bright-yellow plastic flashlights, batteries included. With assistance from his gold Zippo, Hector managed to find the upturned flashlight display. He heard the moaning once again.

Crawling on his hands and knees through the chaos, he moved stealthily toward Ellen's groans, occasionally shining the light in a wide, sweeping arch. After several minutes, he located Ellen buried beneath a mound of shelving.

"It's okay, little girl, it's okay," he whispered in a soothing voice. "Hector's here, baby girl. Hector will take care of you."

Hector stood and began sweeping the light over the rumble of the store floor. The light stopped on a package of baby wipes. He carefully swabbed the wipes against Ellen's forehead, which now carried a large bruise and tiny cut.

"You're okay, baby girl," he whispered. "It's all over, and you're okay." Hector leaned down, gently kissing Ellen on the lips.

Weinstein arrived shortly after the storm, followed by several Mexicans in a battered pickup truck loaded down with sheets of plywood.

"It's a disaster!" he cried. "Why me? Why does this happen to an honest man?" Then he stopped, opened the cash register, emptied its contents, and allowed a brief smile. "Thank the Lord for good insurance!" The store would be closed for several weeks.

Unbelievably, Hector's Super Sport Chevy did not have a scratch. He helped Ellen in after Weinstein gave her twenty bucks and requested that she call him in a few days.

Hector drove from the scene, heading south toward Miss Purdy's rooming house.

"Oh my God," Ellen murmured in utter horror. "It's gone—the house is gone!" As was Miss Purdy Whiteside, the Wichita Witch.

The house had vanished in the storm, along with the old maid that owned it. Ellen wondered if Miss Purdy was now in heaven, or possibly hell.

"Better yet," she muttered, "maybe the witch is in Oz!" Then she began to laugh and cry simultaneously.

"Hold on now, girl. It'll be okay." Hector placed his muscular arm around her shoulder. "What's to cry about, baby girl? We're alive!"

"Alive?" Ellen sobbed. "I don't have a job! I don't have a place to live! What little I own is blown to hell! Alive? Who gives a damn?"

"Hey, baby, Hector Rodriguez is here, and I swear it will get better. Trust me, baby girl."

The Spanish neighborhood where Hector lived had not been touched by the tornado, although at first sight Ellen thought it might have taken a direct hit.

Hector's house sat in what looked like the world's largest weed garden, and the lawn and driveway were filled with stripped-down cars. As dismal the outside appearance was, the inside took her back. Everything in the house looked new—leather furniture, big screen TVs, a stereo system that covered one long wall, and red velvet everywhere.

"You like, baby girl?" Hector made a sweeping motion with his right arm, smiling as they surveyed years of professional stealing.

"It's beautiful," Ellen said in sincere awe.

Still trembling with shock and dismay, Ellen drank six beers that night. It was her first experience drinking alcohol. It would also be her first time with a man.

Hector watched from the doorway the following morning. His face clearly radiated something special. Call it pride, or call it love, Hector Rodriguez had never slept with a virgin before, and this was a fact he treasured.

For the next three months, Ellen truly believed she must have died and gone to heaven. Hector waited on her as if she were a princess—lavish gifts, fresh flowers daily, and she nearly died when he brought home the red Corvette.

But at six months, things began to change. Ellen, now three months pregnant, would not see Hector for days at a time. He would become angry when questioned.

"Get off my back, you Gringo whore," was his most frequent response. "I got you and now a kid to take care of. I'm not here because I work at nights. You got that, Senorita white trash?"

The Wichita Sheriff's Department confiscated Ellen's red Corvette. Hector awaited trial on car theft and interstate trafficking. She had no place to go and no way to get there—the story of her life.

Hector changed from loving to domineering. He, of course, maintained his pride and told all his friends that his woman was a virgin and his son would be called the little macho man.

Unfortunately for Hector, Ellen gave birth to a beautiful baby girl. She named her daughter Pamela Sue, in remembrance of her best friend in high school, who died tragically of a drug overdose. After the baby was born, Hector went from domineering to monstrous. The verbal abuse she could handle, but no man would beat her, something Hector seemed to enjoy with regularity.

Late one Saturday night, Hector arrived home drunk and high on cocaine.

"Where you been all day?" His voice was menacing.

"Where do you think, Hector?" Ellen shot back. "I have no car, no money, no job, no nothing. So just where in the hell do you think I've been?"

Hector rushed across the room like an attacking tiger, hitting her in the face, breaking her nose. "Don't ever talk to me like that again, bitch!"

Ellen ran to the bedroom, trying hard to breathe as she choked on blood. She pulled the Smith and Wesson .357 Magnum from the nightstand as Hector entered the room in a rage.

"Touch me again, you bastard, and I'll kill you!"

"You'll kill me?" Hector's laugh was satanic. I'll kill you, whore!" he hissed. "And your white-trash daughter!" In a flash, Hector produced the six-inch switchblade.

He took one step, and Ellen closed her eyes, pulling the trigger of the big handgun six times. Wood cracked and splintered as the slugs whizzed around the room. The third shot hit Hector in the shoulder, nearly tearing his arm off.

He cried out in pain, dropping the knife as he fell to the floor. Ellen stood over him, enraged. "If you ever come near me or my daughter again, Hector Rodriguez, I swear by all that's holy, you will be a dead man!"

Ellen spit in his face and went to the next room to get her daughter.

The police called the incident self-defense. Two weeks later, Hector was convicted for car theft and sentenced to three years in state prison.

Before Ellen walked out the night of the shooting, she took the shoebox that contained seven thousand dollars from the freezer. She had earned it.

Now, three years later, Ellen Pearson laughed as she watched a fumbling Tom Tabor attempt to flip round waffles on the hot grill. Tom laughed as well but quickly turned solemn as their eyes met in that special way. Tom wondered if he might possibly be falling in love.

Neither could see the black Mercedes with tinted windows parked across the highway.

"You owe me big time, bitch, and I'm here to collect!" Hector hissed through clenched teeth.

The Letter: August 14

||||||||||||||||||||||||||||||||||||||||||||||||||||||||||||||||||||||||||

Recently, it has become extremely hard to fall asleep at night. The warden allowed me to have a small lamp in my cell, and from about six o'clock until the wee hours, I study the Bible you gave me. There is so much to think about, and I find myself almost losing consciousness in the red words of Christ.

Two statements that will not leave me alone, "You shall call his name Jesus, for he will save his people from their sins."

Oh, how I wish he could forgive me, Tina. The love and tenderness of Jesus always leaves me feeling that much worse. How could I ever call myself one of his people? Why would the Son of God forgive such an evil person?

I'm beginning to see the whole picture clearly now. Yes, there are "his people," and yes, I believe Jesus will save them for all eternity. On the other hand, there are those like me that almost cer-

tainly belong to Satan, and yes, the evil one will carry his people to hell for all eternity.

That brings me to the second verse that stays in my mind twenty-four hours a day: "Do not be afraid any longer." And you know, Tina, I no longer am afraid. If I've learned anything in my Bible study, it's that God is fair and his justice will be honest. My sins are many and of the worst nature. So would it be fair and honest justice served if I asked for forgiveness? I don't think so. Therefore, I am not afraid any longer, and I hope God sees that I am ready to pay for my sins. It's the way it should be, and I must prove to God that I am man enough to take what punishment is due me.

You see, Tina, I might feel differently if at some point earlier in my life I had committed to Christ. But unfortunately, the lock Satan had on me was strong and ever present.

There was a time, however, that I truly believe God opened a saving door for me. What did I do? I slammed it in the face of God!

After I took the job as cook at the Waffle House, my relationship with Ellen developed quickly. I can't say it was love as I know love for you, but I did care deeply for her and Pammy.

We started going to church together, I nearly stopped drinking, and we even discussed what it might be like to be married. I guess that was the happiest I'd been in many a year.

It was during that period of time that I believe God opened the door for me one Sunday morning, but I was a coward and refused the calling. Maybe if I had listened to God, things might have been different. Just maybe if I had, I would not have committed another terrible sin.

The Seventh Sin

After six weeks, Tom could fry eggs, cook bacon, and toast waffles with the best of them. He found a great deal of pride in holding down a steady job. Tom rarely drank whiskey now, and his ulcer seemed to have almost disappeared.

"Here's your paycheck, Mr. Tabor." Ellen's smile said more than that.

"Thank you kindly, Miss Pearson. It is indeed an honor to work for such an understanding, and, uh, beautiful boss." Both Tom and Ellen blushed.

"Well then, Tom, with all the overtime you're working, what are you gonna do with the money?"

"Let's see, what to do now that I'm rich?" Ellen laughed at his statement. "I need a couple pairs of jeans, maybe three or four new tee shirts, and yes, I might just buy me a pair of name-brand tennis shoes!"

Ellen really liked this honest man and felt a strange kinship, as if sensing they both had walked bitter paths filled with disappointment and loneliness.

"That's it?" Ellen attempted mock surprise. "Jeans and tee shirts?"

"And tennis shoes!" Tom poured them both a cup of freshly brewed coffee.

He lowered his head in contemplation. "Uh, Ellen."

"Yes, Tom?"

"There is one other thing." Ellen could see that he was nervous.

"I'm supposed to look at an apartment today. It ain't much but a heck of a lot better than my truck-stop motel room."

"That's great, Tom!"

"Well, great it ain't, but at least it will be more like a real home." Tom lowered his head again as he held tightly to the hot coffee mug. "I was wondering if maybe you'd take a look at it with me. You know, get a woman's opinion."

Ellen's blue-green eyes sparkled as she pushed a large honey-gold ringlet of hair back from her forehead. "That's very nice of you to ask, Tom. Not many men in my life ever cared if I had an opinion."

"Well, I suppose you must have known some really stupid men."

"Bingo!" Ellen reached out, touching Tom's strong forearm. "Tell ya what, my superstar employee, I would be honored to offer my professional feminine opinion on one condition."

"Name it!" Tom's happiness filled his face.

"After we look at your new place, you have to come over to the house and have supper with Pammy and me. Is it a deal?"

Tom's eyes moistened. "Nothing in this world could make me happier."

After supper, Tom played Monopoly with Pammy while Ellen washed the dishes. He watched the beautiful child laugh and squeal as he landed on Park Place, her property. For a moment, Tom felt like he needed to run, to hide, to find a dark and quiet place. As he watched the child so pretty and bright, he remembered Baby, his sister, the little life he had smothered.

"Okay, guys, ready for ice cream and cake?"

"Yes, Mommy, yes!" Pammy jumped to her feet and reached out for Tom's hand. "Come on, Mister Tom; Mommy makes the bestest cake in the world."

After dessert, Tom quietly got up to leave. "Thanks for the great dinner, Ellen. Quite honestly, I'm a little tired of bacon and eggs."

"You're very welcome, Tom. Let's do it again soon."

"And good night to you, Miss Pammy. Thanks for teaching me how to lose at Monopoly."

"You're welcome, Mister Tom," the little girl said cheerfully and then surprised him by placing her arms around his neck and kissing him on the cheek. It was all Tom could do to maintain his composure at that moment.

"Okay, little one, go put on your jammies. Mommy will come tuck you in shortly."

"Good night, Mister Tom; come back and see me!"

"Good night, angel," Tom whispered in response.

"Well, thanks again, Ellen, it really was—"

Ellen placed both hands against his cheeks, gently kissing him on the lips. "No, thank you, Tom. It's nice to have a real man around."

Tom walked the mile stretch back to the motel feeling as if he might be in the dream of his life. No one heard him singing the old James Taylor tune "You've Got a Friend." And no one saw the black Mercedes parked in the darkness three doors down from Ellen's small, wood frame house.

"So you done got yourself a boyfriend." Hector's voice poured out venomous hostility. "You owe me, tramp, and payback time is drawing near." He did the third line of cocaine for the evening.

Tom scrubbed the grill, and Ellen sat at the counter, calculating the day's receipts.

"So what you got planned for Sunday, Tom—anything?"

"Same ol', same ol'," Tom responded with his back to her. "Get up, read the paper, watch a ballgame. You know, all that man stuff."

"How 'bout you go to church with Pammy and me?" Tom did not respond. "Afterward, we can have a picnic down by the lake. Maybe go for a swim."

Ellen did not see the single tear stream slowly down his face.

"Ellen, I'd love to go to church with you and Pammy."

"Great! Do you know where the Nazarene Church is over by the Putt-Putt?"

"Yeah, we passed it on the way in, right?"

"Sure did. Want me to pick you up at your apartment?"

"No thanks, Ellen. I'm supposed to buy a car after work today."

"That's great news, Tom! What kind of car is it?"

"Well, it has an engine, four tires, steering wheel, brakes, I think, and one heck of a lot of rust. It ain't pretty, but the price is right, and I'm sure as heck tired of walking everywhere I go!" Tom would purchase the junk heap without a bill of sale, insurance, or driver's license, all of which were unattainable in his present state.

Ellen wondered if she might be falling seriously in love with this gentle, humble man.

Tom fought back the overwhelming guilt from the first moment he entered the church until the closing altar call.

The young minister finished the sermon about Christ forgiving sins if people would only ask.

"Please turn to page fifty-two and join me in singing 'Amazing Grace.'" The preacher looked out at Tom.

Tom did not sing along; he couldn't. He knew if he even opened his mouth, all the years of torture, agony, pain, guilt, and sin would scream out for redemption.

"Amazing Grace, how sweet the sound that saved a wretch like me. I once was lost but now I'm found, was blind, but now I see."

Tom thought the words might just rupture his heart.

Ellen grasped Tom's hand in hers and squeezed tightly. She then looked into his tear-filled eyes and saw unbelievable pain.

"Tom, I have to find Jesus. Will you go with me?"

"I can't, Ellen." He choked back his anguish. "I'm not worthy."

"I love you, Tom," Ellen whispered before walking to the altar with her head held high. Little Pammy followed her mother down the aisle.

Tom literally ran from the church, sobbing as if he'd just lost his sanity, crying out in woeful suffering. He sat in his four-door rusted Volkswagen, cursing in frustration outside the quick stop. It would be another fifteen minutes before he could buy beer this beautiful Sunday morning, and he needed a drink like never before.

With a case of cold Pabst Blue Ribbon loaded in the back seat, Tom drove east like the devil was behind him. Of course, Satan wasn't behind him; he sat smiling in the passenger's seat.

Ellen felt like a new woman, as if the weight of the world had been lifted from her freckled shoulders. She was forgiven. She was a Christian now.

"Where'd Mister Tom go, Mommy? Are we still going to have our picnic?"

"I guess it was just too hard for him, honey, but Tom is a good man, and Jesus will bring him back."

"I hope so, Mommy. I like Mister Tom a lot."

"I do too, baby. Yes, I do too."

Ellen went straight to Tom's apartment and then to the Waffle House. He was nowhere to be found. *I bet he's calmed down now and is waiting for us at the lake,* she thought, or rather, hoped.

Ellen cruised the lake for nearly an hour before laying out the blanket for a lonely picnic with her little girl.

Tom drove the old Volkswagen down a secluded country road, eventually pulling off next to an old termite-infested barn just waiting for a good wind to bring it down. For the next eight hours, he drank beer, cursed God, and cried like a baby.

Ellen tucked Pammy in bed and read her the Bible story about Noah's ark. After the child fell asleep, Ellen went to the kitchen and began to read her Bible and thank the Lord for her many blessings.

She raised her head from prayer as the sound of a distant car door closing got her attention.

"Tom," she whispered in hopeful anticipation.

Ellen ran from the kitchen at the first knock on the door. "Tom? Oh, Tom, thank God you're here!"

Her knees buckled, and she felt like she might faint as the door opened to the twisted, evil face of one Hector Rodriguez.

"Tom," he mocked. "Oh, God, please let it be Tommy. Well I guess you're out of luck, 'cause Hector's home and its' time for payback!"

Ellen arched her back, coiling for an attack. "You get outta here right now, Hector, or I swear I'll call the police."

Hector laughed in such an evil way that Ellen's body chilled to the bone. "I mean it, Hector! Get out of here now before I call—"

His fist crashed into her face like a sledgehammer, knocking her over the couch, facedown, into the cheap coffee table that exploded in razor sharp shards of glass.

Hector sprang upon her like a wild animal, turning her over on her back. Ellen's face was now a mass of blood from numerous deep cuts.

"You ain't so pretty now, are you, baby girl?"

Ellen, nearly unconscious, managed to bring up her knee with a burst of power, catching Hector in the groin. He fell back onto the couch, moaning as he cupped both hands around his private parts.

"Aaaaahhh!" he screamed. "You've had it now, bitch." He pulled out the switchblade and with a single motion produced the glimmering steel, waving it just under Ellen's blood-filled eyes.

"Oh, dear God, I pray…" Ellen's speech sounded guttural as the blood ran into her throat. "Please protect Pammy."

"God ain't here, bitch! Tommy ain't here either. All you got is Hector Rodriguez, and time's up!"

Hector wrapped her blood-soaked hair tightly in his left hand and pulled her head back violently, exposing her soft, white neck.

"Mommy, Mommy." Pammy's shrills filled the room. "Leave my mommy alone!"

The child ran at Hector without fear, flailing her tiny arms like a windmill in a windstorm. "Don't hurt my mommy!"

Caught off guard, filled with rage, and high on crack cocaine, Hector leaned back with his right hand sticking out. The child ran directly into the six-inch blade, which sliced through fragile ribs, puncturing her heart. In a matter of seconds, the beautiful, little child that just this morning had gone before the altar died like a slaughtered lamb.

With that, Hector leaned over and slit Ellen's throat.

Tom didn't know what he would or could say. All he knew for sure was that he loved Ellen and her little girl. He would apologize, and he would return to church and ask for God's forgiveness. He swore to heaven that there would be no more sins.

He wondered why a black Mercedes was parked along the street in front of Ellen's home. When Tom noticed the door open, panic gripped his heart.

"Ellen? Ellen?" His terror became almost overwhelming. "Are you okay?" he whispered.

Tom stood in absolute horror as his eyes looked upon the unholy carnage before him. Pammy lay awkwardly against the couch with eyes open, filled with fright, and her pink pajamas covered in blood.

Frozen in place, Tom looked down upon the woman he loved and could hardly recognize her.

The sound that came up and out of Tom could never be reproduced or imagined in your most hideous nightmare. It was a cry from the pits of hell. Even Hector became terrorized by the screams of insanity before him.

Tom leaped like an angel of Satan, falling on Hector with uncontainable hatred.

Hector slashed at Tom in desperation, cutting his chest, face, and left arm. Tom did not feel the pain. With both hands holding Hector's knife-wielding arm, Tom snapped it like a winter twig. He then began to beat the murderer with his fist until Hector's face looked like sanguinary pulp.

As the Mexican pleaded for his life, Tom wrapped both hands tightly around his neck and began a slow, crushing motion of unholy power. He could hear cracking and sucking sounds as Hector's life ended in one final gurgling gasp.

"I'll see you again in hell," Tom hissed through his twisted lips.

Those would be the last words Thomas Lavon Tabor would speak.

The Crazy Place

IIIIIIIIIIIIIIIIIIIIIIIIIIIIIIIIIIIIIIIIIIIIIIIIIIIIIIIIIIIIIIII

When the police arrived, they found Tom in the front lawn, nearly dead from the numerous wounds Hector inflicted before his own execution.

Tom lay in the wet grass with arms reaching out to each side and his legs stretched straight with feet crossed. It almost looked like a crucifixion. Barely conscious, his eyes remained open and wide. The police and medics attempted to communicate but received zero response from the severely wounded man.

After several weeks, the detectives surmised that Hector killed Ellen and her child. It looked pretty clear that Tom arrived on the scene after the murders of Ellen and Pammy.

Tom Tabor did not go to court, as the police ruled Hector's death self-defense on Tom's part. They did, however, keep Tom in lockup, hoping to hear his story, but Tom Tabor did not speak a solitary word.

After several psychologists attempted to bring Tom out of his stupor, the district judge followed their instructions and placed Tom in a mental institution for further examination.

Thomas Tabor walked into the locked ward of the John B. Cook Mental Institute wrapped tightly in a straightjacket. No one could be sure if he was dangerous, but for whatever reason, everyone feared him.

Doctor Kirk, the police psychologist, entered the office of the institute's chief psychiatrist, Doctor Benjamin Golic.

"Well, Doctor Golic," Kirk began, "I really can't tell you with certainty if Mr. Tabor is perilous. I do know, however, that the way in which he murdered Hector Rodriguez can only be described as insanely brutal, to say the least."

"Has he been violent since the incident?"

"No, I can't say violent, but he can look at you, Doctor, in such a way, that it's … it's … hard to put into words."

"Like how, Doctor Kirk?"

"Well, I'm not a religious man, but if I were, I'd describe his look like that of Satan himself!"

"I see. What is your prognosis on his refusal to speak?"

"Can't say with certainty, Doctor—unholy trauma, to be sure. It must have sent him into shock too deep to imagine. Have you seen the police photos?"

"Yes, I have. The worst I've ever witnessed. Anything you can tell me that might help in our evaluation of Mr. Tabor?"

"Just one thing more. Do you have any ministers or priests around here?"

"Yes, occasionally we find that people of faith have a unique gift in breaking through the barriers a lot of our patients build around their true emotions."

"Well, I'll give you this warning, sir. Don't allow any people of the religious persuasion near this guy. We thought like you and attempted to have a local priest meet with Tabor. You know, see if we could break the ice, get the guy to speak. We really wanted to hear his side of the murders."

"Did the priest help?"

"It was really weird, Doctor Golic; the priest didn't spend maybe five minutes with Tabor."

"And?"

"Father O'Malley came from Tabor's cell white as a sheet. Almost terrified! He didn't say much other than Tabor was a devil and we better damn well keep him locked up."

"Strange," Doctor Golic said. "Well, I believe we'll keep Mr. Tabor in isolation for a few months. What medication would you suggest?"

"The strongest stuff you have, Doctor. In all honesty, this guy really scares me, and I have worked with some pretty sick criminals in my time."

"Thank you, Doctor Kirk. I'll make sure our staff keeps Mr. Tabor heavily sedated and at arms' length."

———

Patient 102 sat in the corner of the padded room, looking out intensely as if constantly reliving the hideous murders of Ellen and Pammy.

Doctor Golic watched the patient via the closed-circuit television, along with nurse Lillian Flek.

"So what do you think, Lillian? Is the man a menace?"

"I really don't think so, Doctor. He's been almost motionless for weeks now. All the poor man does is sit in the corner and stare off as if watching hell revealed."

"Has he attempted to communicate to anyone, Nurse?"

"No, not really communicate, Doctor. But he can look at you in such a way that you feel like he's trying to express the horror of his life. It's not frightening, Doctor Golic. His expression is tragic."

"I see. You think it would be in his best interest to move him into the general ward?"

"Yes, sir, I do. I've worked around him for six months now, and I do not believe he is a danger to himself or to anyone else."

"Okay then, Lillian. I trust your judgment. Let's move him downstairs tomorrow."

"Any other instructions, sir?"

"Yes, let's cut back his medication gradually and give him a little freedom to move about."

"I believe he might surprise us, Doctor Golic."

"Let's hope so. Um, one more thing."

"Yes, sir?"

"Try to test his IQ, if possible, and make sure an orderly is with him anytime he's outside of his room."

"Should I room him with anyone?"

"Yes, company might do him good; maybe bring him out of his shell. Put Mr. Tabor with Tom Hunter—he never shuts up!"

"Great idea, Doctor Golic. One patient that never speaks and one that never stops!"

The next morning, Nurse Flek entered the padded room with Leon, the very big orderly.

"Good morning, Tom. How are you feeling today?" Like most days, Tom Tabor looked off into the twilight zone. Nurse Flek watched him carefully. "Would you like to leave this room and move to an area where other people are?"

Tom slowly turned to face the nurse. His expression remained stoic, but she saw a sparkle in his eyes like never before.

"So could you say, 'Yes, Lillian, I'd like to be around some new people'?"

Tom did not flinch, but his expression brightened dramatically. "Come on then, Tom. Let's go have breakfast and meet some new people."

Nurse Flek met Doctor Golic later in the day. "Doctor, you are going to be absolutely amazed at the turnaround with Thomas Tabor."

"How so?"

"Well, Doctor, I spent the entire day with him. We ate breakfast, walked around the grounds, spent time in the whirlpool, and he even picked up a *National Geographic* magazine and appeared to be reading it."

"That is indeed terrific news, Nurse. Maybe there's hope for this unfortunate lad."

Nurse Flek walked Tom to his new room, the one he'd be sharing with Tom Hunter, or the Mad Hatter, as the staff called him. "Tom Tabor, this is your roommate Tom Hunter."

"Well, kiss my country backside, boy; we've got the same first name. Glad to meet ya. Glad to meet ya. Glad to meet ya!" Hunter had the habit of repeating himself often.

Tom Tabor looked quizzically at the little guy who oddly reminded him of Popeye the Sailor Man. Nurse Flek thought she might have seen the slightest smile upon Tabor's lips.

Tom slowly walked over to the large window with bars and peered out into the beautiful fall day. Little Tom ran over, twisted his head sideways, and looked up and around the large man.

"Do you like to play golf? I like to golf. I like to golf. I like to golf. Hole in one. Hole in one. Hole in one!"

"Now, Mr. Hunter, why don't you allow your new roommate a little time to adjust to his new environment."

"Okay, okay, okay, okay, but I'm not crazy. I'm not crazy. I'm not crazy."

Nurse Flek did not see Thomas Tabor smiling as he looked out the window.

That night, Tom lay quietly upon the cotton sheets, thinking about Tina. He also thought about his family and how he'd murdered five people. His eyes moistened as the picture of Ellen and Pammy bought back the horror of the worst night in his life.

"I have a lawnmower!" Little Tom blurted out. "I cut grass, cut grass, cut grass."

Tom ignored the Mad Hatter's ramblings and wondered why the staff tagged this crazy little guy with such a nickname. Was he still living in a real world or falling down an endless hole like Alice in Wonderland?

"Stole the mower; it ain't mine. Ain't mine. Ain't mine."

Little Tom got out of bed and crouched on the floor, walking around like a dog. "Want a puppy? I got puppies! Lots of puppies—big puppies, big puppies, big puppies."

Tom rose slowly and gave the Mad Hatter a look that caused the little man to leap into bed and pull the covers over his head. He did not say another word the rest of the night.

Doctor Golic stood just outside the doorway, watching Tom Tabor meticulously glue the cut pieces of wood into a magnificent birdhouse.

"He's good with his hands, isn't he?" The doctor spoke softly.

"Yes, he is, sir." Nurse Flek smiled. "And from his test, Doctor, Thomas Tabor has a very high IQ."

"Do you think he's crazy, Nurse?"

"No, sir, I don't."

"Based on?"

"Based on the fact that he has not disobeyed one rule, he reads everything he gets his hands on, he's industrious, and the children."

"The children?"

"Yes, sir. Several weeks ago, after I'd spent some time with Tom outside, we walked by the music room. He stopped and listened for the longest period until little Sara walked over, looked up into his eyes, and clasped his hand."

"What did Tabor do?"

"He smiled, Doctor."

Doctor Golic also smiled at this news.

"Then Tom followed Sara into the music room, and all the children circled around him like they saw something special in him we can't. Now he's in the music room every day, with all the children holding him, touching him, loving him, Doctor."

"Remarkable."

"Yes, sir, it is, and no, sir, this man is not crazy. He's just turned inside himself. I believe he has decided not to deal with the evil of the world anymore. The children sense that."

"Very well then, Nurse. Let's give Mr. Tabor until the end of the month. If all goes well, I'll call Richard at the Freedom Placement Center. Maybe if Mr. Tabor can gradually work himself back into society, no matter how crazy it truly is, he can face reality and speak again."

"He'll make it, Doctor. I'm sure of it."

"Let's hope you are right, Nurse."

Tom stood on the stoop of the John B. Cook Mental Institute tightly grasping the olive green gym bag in his right hand. It contained two pairs of blue jeans, three white tee shirts, and a pair of Nike tennis shoes.

"Good Luck, Mr. Tabor." Doctor Golic reached out his hand to shake, and Tom responded in kind. "I look forward to seeing you again. Maybe we can have a long talk someday." The doctor could not be sure, but he believed Tom almost smiled.

"Good-bye, Tom, and good luck!" Nurse Lillian Flek stood on tiptoes and kissed Tom on the cheek. She could have sworn he said "I love you" with only his eyes.

Tom turned, wiped the single tear from his eye, and walked twenty paces to the blue van that read, "Hopewell Freedom Placement Center—Bringing Hope to Those That Want to Work."

The Letter: August 17

IIIIIIIIIIIIIIIIIIIIIIIIIIIIIIIIIIIIIIIIIIIIIIIIIIIIIIIII

I didn't get a chance to write you the past two days because, oddly enough, I just couldn't stop reading the Bible you gave me. For whatever reason, my focus is transfixed on the Apostle Paul. It's like I relate to him. Before God blinded Saul, this guy did some pretty terrible things, even being involved in the murder of Christians! So what's the relationship between the Apostle Paul and me? We were both murderers. God punished us both.

And I guess the comparison stops there. As you know, Paul went on to be a great leader and to spread the Word of God far and wide. He changed, and God gave him the opportunity to atone for his sins. That makes sense to me. Unfortunately, even if I could be forgiven, there is no atonement for Thomas Tabor. In fourteen days, I will begin payment for living with the devil all my life. It's sad, but it's fair. God's perfect justice.

After I left the crazy place, life seemed to go on as if I were caught in a dream I couldn't escape from. Tina, did you ever have a nightmare where you were absolutely terrified and tried with all your might to scream, but no sound would come out? Well, that pretty well describes me. It had been nearly two years since I had spoken a word to anyone, and it was as if I had forgotten how to talk.

Once, after I'd been at the Hopewell Center for several days, I tried to speak. It was in the wee hours of the morning, and all the pitiful residents of the center were still asleep. I awoke, went to my tiny sink, splashed cold water on my face, and looked at myself in the mirror. I tried to speak. I formed the word hello on my lips and in my mind, but no sound came out. I don't know what happened to me the night Ellen and little Pammy were murdered, but even if I wanted to, I no longer could speak a single word. I sometimes wonder if God took my voice like he did Paul's sight.

You know, I really hated the mental hospital, although I cared for Nurse Flek and Doctor Golic. Everybody there was truly crazy, and I often wondered if you could catch craziness like some kind of disease.

Hopewell was different in a lot of ways. All the people there were mentally handicapped but cognizant of all that was going on. In some cases, the little people, as I thought of them, were a heck of a lot smarter than the staff, of which most were government-paid morons.

The center gave me peace and quiet. No one really bothered me, although I did not much care for being treated like an idiot. The place brought me security and I guess a certain tranquility. I could be alone, and that was just fine with everyone.

I sometimes thought of the center as a big can of cheap mixed nuts. You know, the kind you buy at K-Mart with some off-brand label. You think, Oh boy, a big can of all kinds of tasty, expensive nuts, until you open the can and find mostly peanuts. You dig and dig through the greasy contents, pushing the peanuts over the edge until you find that one big whole cashew!

Sounds funny, doesn't it? And I guess it was. The center seemed like a big can of peanuts, and I was the only cashew.

For whatever reason, I became the leader, the protector, and the father figure in the can of nuts known as the Hopewell Center.

The Hopewell Center

The Hopewell Center stood peacefully just outside the small Kansas town of Great Bend. Years prior, the main building housed the production facility for a large oil rig supply company. When the oil and gas exploration business died in the Midwest, the company went bust and the federal government purchased the land and buildings.

Sometime in the early seventies, the government decided to transform the place into a training and placement center for mentally handicapped people.

Thomas Tabor knew with great certainty that he was neither crazy nor retarded. He just couldn't speak. Because of his inability to talk, everyone just assumed that Tom must be slow- witted, stupid, or severely intellectually limited. Truth be told, Tom liked the game. It left him with no demands beyond sleeping, eating, and watching cartoons.

When Tom first arrived, the staff herded the group of five new arrivals into the conference room.

"Good morning!" the short, fat, bald-headed man greeted the new collection of little people, as Tom also came to call this new group that he wanted so badly to protect. The greeter and director of The Hopewell Center always called the residents his "little people." Once he was asked by a government stuffed shirt inspector as to why he referred to these poor souls as "little people," as if the term itself was derogatory. "Well, Inspector," his smile thoughtful and sincere, "they want little, they demand little, they worry little. To me they are like Peter Pan and the Lost Boys; full of joy and happiness, taking great pleasure in the little things all us never notice."

Homer grunted like a captured pig. Bernice said, "Good morning to you." Tom and Larry said nothing, and Barb shouted, "Go to hell, you bald-headed turd!"

Tom smiled at Barb's greeting as the fat, little administrator frowned and pulled at his too-tight vest, no doubt purchased off the rack at a two-for-one men's clothing store.

"Yes, well, my name is Alex Q. Pumpernickel, the third."

Barb laughed as if disgusted. "You got three pumpernickels? Stupid!"

Pumpernickel stared at Barb with great contempt. "Now listen here, young lady."

"Young lady?" Barb squished her face as if made of flexible rubber. "Hell, boy, I'm fifty years old! Old baldy's stupid, ain't he!"

Mr. Pumpernickel sent a cold, expecting look toward Julie, one of the Hopewell Center's counselors. The young, seriously overweight supervisor immediately pulled a chair up behind Barb.

"Now, you must be quiet and respectful toward Mr. Pumpernickel, or you won't get cookies and Kool-Aid after the welcome session."

Barb gave this serious thought. "What kind of cookies?"

"Oatmeal and raisin," Julie responded.

"Okay, I'll shut up." Barb twisted her face into a wrinkled ball once again.

"Very good!" Pumpernickel unconsciously pulled at his pinstriped vest again. "Now, before I tell you about our wonderful home here at Hopewell and what great things you'll be doing, let's go around the room and have each of you tell the group your name."

"Hello, my name is Bernice Camary. I want to be a dancer."

"I want to be a watermelon," Barb said under her breath.

"And your name, sir?" The administrator looked at Tom.

Tom smiled, mostly out of humor with the situation, and wrote upon the small square blackboard Nurse Flek gave him before he left the crazy place, "Tom Tabor—I cannot speak."

Tom turned slowly from side to side so that all the little people could read it. Bernice smiled beautifully, and Barb stuck her gray, film-coated tongue out as far as it would stretch.

Larry grunted several indistinguishable words, pounded upon the table, and hid his face behind his arms. Then Larry farted, and the little people erupted in laughter. Even Tom smiled, shaking his head.

"His name is Larry Sanders, and he doesn't speak much," Julie interjected.

"Hell, get the turd a blackboard like Tom over there," Barb shouted and once again stuck her tongue out in Tom's direction. It was Barb's way of flirting.

"My name is Homer Diggs. I can read."

"Big deal," Barb whispered.

"And?" Pumpernickel pulled again at his vest. "What's your name?"

"Bar Bar A. That's my name, ask me again I'll tell you the same!" The little people erupted once again.

Red in the face, the administrator spoke. "Do you have a last name, Bar Bar A?"

"Yeah, I got a last name." She smiled broadly, showing all four of her teeth. "I am Barbara the Third, just like you! Hey, baldy, maybe we're related."

Tom knew this place was most assuredly going to be a kick.

Pumpernickel walked to the side of the room where a flip chart hung upon a wooden tripod.

"Now then, group, what you can expect at the Hopewell Center—"

"Where the hell are the cookies?" Barb asked Julie, clearly annoyed.

"We'll get cookies in a little bit, Barb. Now just sit here and listen."

Larry farted again.

Barb laughed loudly as she ran her fingers through her Don King hairdo. "Sounds like Larry's been a eatin' bean cookies."

Larry grunted and hid his face.

"Julie, does Larry need to go to the bathroom?" Pumpernickel asked, clearly annoyed.

"No! No! No!" Larry shouted and beat the table with both hands.

"Sounds like he already did!" Barb interjected.

"Smells like it too!" Homer added.

"Julie, can you please control these people?"

"Yes, sir. Sorry, Mr. Pumpernickel."

"Where the hell's the cookies and Kool-Aid at, anyhow?" Barb's four bottom teeth pushed out, making her look like the US Marine Corps mascot.

"Get the woman a cookie, for goodness sakes!" Pumpernickel pulled at his vest.

"Thank you, Mr. Third." Barb smiled as if everything would be just wonderful now.

"All right now, is everybody happy?"

"Yes, sir." Bernice spoke softly in a childlike voice. Homer shook his head up and down as Larry grunted acknowledgment. Barb stuck her cookie-covered tongue out at Tom.

Pumpernickel flipped the first white page back on the tripod.

"Welcome to the Hopewell Center, where people want to work. Our job at Hopewell is, first and foremost, to find each of you a job. Each of you will be assigned a room with a partner."

Barb looked at Tom with a gigantic grin as she raised both eyebrows high on her rubbery forehead. Tom, in turn, winked at Barb, which caused her to blush.

"We will provide you with living quarters, three meals a day, and many wonderful social activities."

"Like what?" Barb inquired.

"Like pizza night!" Julie stated enthusiastically.

"I hate pizza," Barb shot back.

"Once a month we have dances." Julie was now talking directly to Barb.

"I love to dance," Bernice spoke softly.

"I hate to dance," Barb retorted. "Do you play spin the bottle?" Barb gave Tom a quick cookie-crumb smile.

"No!" Pumpernickel fired back. "Any sexual contact of any kind will result in those involved being placed in detention."

"Poop!" Barb whispered.

Pumpernickel knew that Barb would be a problem. "We will attempt to find each of you a job outside the Hopewell Center, working for different local companies. Fifty percent of your earnings will go to pay for your food and board. Twenty-five percent will be placed in a savings account and utilized for clothing, medical and dental expenses, and emergencies."

Larry farted again.

"Hey, sounds like Larry has an emergency!" Barb added, and the little people once again broke into great laughter.

Tom wrote on his blackboard, "What happens to the other 25 percent?"

"Good question, Mr. Tabor!" Pumpernickel wondered if Tom just might be the brightest of this new group. "You all get to keep that twenty-five percent and utilize it any way you wish."

Tom began to contemplate how he'd get whiskey into the Center.

Pumpernickel continued. "Once you are placed in a job, Julie will check on your progress daily. If you do not behave and work hard, you will not be allowed out of the Center, and you will work in the pillow barn."

"What the hell's that?" Barb asked incredulously.

"We stuff and sew pillows for the federal prisons," Pumpernickel said.

"Sounds like a turd-face job," Barb retorted.

"Exactly." Pumpernickel smiled. "So do good on the outside."

Tom wrote furiously upon his blackboard. "How do we ever get out of here?"

"Yes!" Pumpernickel pronounced. "Yet another good question, Mr. Tabor. If you do a good job on the outside, behave yourself while here inside the Center, and prove you can take care of yourself, you can move into what we call the Freedom Project."

What a load of government crap, Tom thought to himself.

Tom raised his blackboard. "What is the Freedom Project?"

"After one year of hard work and good behavior, you can be tested by the county mental health agency. If both they and me agree, and your employer is willing to provide full-time employment, you can live on your own, with minimal supervision, of course," the administrator concluded.

Tom swore to himself that he'd be out of this can of nuts in twelve months.

The Hopewell Center remained extremely crowded, as most occupants never made it to the Freedom Project.

After Pumpernickel's governmental analogue of rules and regulations, the new group of little people were assigned rooms. Because of the overcrowding, Tom was placed in a small room with both Larry and Homer. Barb and Bernice went to the east wing, where all the women stayed, and would share an even smaller room.

When Tom entered Room 17, Larry ran past him to the tiny single bed against the window that provided a perfect view of the pillow barn. Larry curled into a ball upon the bed and began to cry.

Homer turned in several slow circles, as if lost in some dark, forbidding forest, before sitting down upon the bottom mattress of the bunk beds across from the small sink. Tom reconciled he'd be sleeping on the top bunk.

The small room, barely furnished, consisted of the beds, sink, and one dresser with three large drawers. Outside the room at thirty paces, Tom found the men's lavatory, which contained five toilet stalls and a community shower with five separate showerheads. In the opposite direction, Tom located the mess hall. Across from the meager dining area, the recreation room maintained numerous children's basic reading books, an old twenty-five-inch TV, and hundreds of simple-looking puzzles.

When Tom returned to Room 17, both Larry and Homer remained exactly like he had left them. They seemed to be frozen in place, locked in time, unable to function without someone leading them.

Homer brought a small plastic suitcase with a huge silver buckle. It sat just inside the door. Larry's total net worth lay in a crumpled laundry bag at the foot of the single bed.

Tom moved about the room as if living with zombies. He carefully unpacked Larry's laundry bag of meager clothing into the top drawer of the orange dresser. At the bottom of the bag, Tom found a very old and frazzled teddy bear missing one button eye. He placed the ragged bear in Larry's arms, and Larry, in turn, clutched the bear to his chest.

Tom watched Homer carefully as he opened the plastic suitcase. Homer remained lost in foreign places Tom hoped never to see. He placed Homer's clothes in the second drawer of the dresser and almost wept as he pulled the tiny book from the suitcase, *The Little Engine That Could*.

Tom thought about his original analogy of the can of mixed nuts. He guessed he was indeed the only cashew of the bunch. Tom vowed at that moment to get away from this place and never again feel sorry for himself. Yes, for the moment, he was a prisoner of society, but he could escape. Poor Homer and Larry would be locked in their world of hopelessness until the day they died.

Tom quietly walked over to Larry's bed, where the poor little guy continued to whimper. He patted Larry on his bony shoulder and pushed his tangled brown hair from his freckled forehead.

Larry slowly reached up with his left hand, strongly clutching Tom's fingers and pulling them down to his chest.

Larry farted and softly whispered, "I'm sorry." Within minutes, Larry found the kind of peace that could only come for him in deep slumber.

Tom remained motionless for a long time as he watched Homer across the room. The poor soul had not moved a muscle for the past two hours. It was eerie, Tom thought. No, not really eerie, it was sad, very sad.

Tom slowly pulled his hand from Larry's chest and walked to the orange dresser, where he fetched Homer's book. He then sat next to Homer and placed his arm across the man-boy's shoulders and laid the book in his lap.

Homer reached down, gently stroking the thin, red book. He then looked up into Tom's eyes and whispered, "Thank you."

Homer stretched out on the bottom bunk, turning his back to Tom while holding the book close to his face. Tom arose from the lower bunk and pulled his toiletry case from the bottom dresser drawer. A hot shower sounded good. As he opened the door to leave Room 17, he heard Homer softly repeating, "I think I can, I think I can."

When Tom returned from the community shower, a place he would later find to be rarely utilized by the other male members at the Hopewell Center, he found both Homer and Larry sound asleep.

Supper would begin in fifteen minutes, so Tom gently woke his new roommates. He motioned with his hands that "the boys," as Tom would later think of them, should wash their face and comb their hair. Both complied, as if Tom were the master of their every move—a fact that quickly became reality.

The first meal for Tom and the boys would prove to be quite similar day after day, month after month—a small portion of dried meat, sometimes hard to recognize, two vegetables, applesauce, and a small piece of flat white cake with crimson icing.

Homer ate slowly and neatly, while Larry seemed more content to utilize his hands and wear half the meal on his shirt. Barb watched Tom's every move throughout the meal until the dessert had been served. She quickly got up and moved in Tom's direction.

Bent over at the waist, severely bowlegged, with pepper hair that looked like she'd just received ten thousand volts, Barb was hard to miss in the dining room setting of thirty little people. At about ten feet from Tom's table, she blurted out, "Hey, turd face, you gonna eat that damn cake?"

Tom smiled, shaking his head at the total insanity of the situation, and held out the cake to Barb.

"Thanks, turd face," she responded before cramming the entire piece of cake into her dirty face.

Larry caught Barb giving his piece of cake the evil eye and began to shout, "No, no, no," as he pounded the table.

Tom placed his arm around Larry's shoulder, and the man-boy instantly calmed down. Homer, in turn, gently patted Tom on the back in a tender gesture. All were at peace until Larry let one go that would have made an elephant proud.

Barb howled with laughter. "Better quit feeding that boy beans!"

Tom formed his hand with two fingers out and made a motion like someone walking. At that moment, both Homer and Larry got up and followed their master to the fenced-in exercise area. Bernice watched them move through the dining room and believed she loved the tall man that the boys followed.

For the next several weeks, the newest group at the Hopewell Center went through a multitude of tests, the purpose being to determine mental aptitude, dexterity, and ability to communicate.

Tom purposefully altered his results to allow the test to show him capable but not altogether normal. Bernice, Barb, and Homer all scored well enough to be considered for outside work placement. Larry scored just below borderline.

After the tests were given and scored, Pumpernickel and Julie once again took the group into the conference room.

Pumpernickel began. "Well now, people, I am so happy and proud of each of you. Let's see here," he said and looked down at the papers in his hand. "Mr. Tabor." Tom thought it odd that the little fat man only called *him* mister and not the other members of the group. In a way, it really pissed him off. "You, sir, have scored the highest test marks in the history of the Hopewell Center!"

Tom smiled and thought, *That's why I'm the cashew in this can of nuts, asshole!*

Pumpernickel continued. "Bernice, Barb, and Homer also placed high enough to be considered for outside work placement."

"Whoop dee doo!" Barb snarled.

Tom watched with mounting concern as Larry clearly realized his name had not been mentioned and seemed ready to launch into a "No! No! No!" response. Tom quickly wrote on his small blackboard, "What about Larry?"

Pumpernickel seemed uncharacteristically nervous. "Well, Mr. Tabor, Larry scored as a potential risk."

With that, Larry let go. "No! No! No!"

The chalk raced across Tom's blackboard. "If Larry doesn't go, I don't go!"

"Well, Mr. Tabor, this is highly irregular! We have rules, procedures, protocol!"

Tom pushed the board high over his head. "Screw your rules!"

Pumpernickel turned beet red, yet for some odd reason he feared the malcontent with the blackboard.

Julie interjected, "Mr. Pumpernickel, if you recall, anytime we place five of our people in a single outside work placement, they must have a full-time staff member present."

"So?" Pumpernickel fired back with tempered indignation.

"So, sir, I received a work order from our friends at Deaton's Laundry. The jobs open in two weeks, and they need five of our people."

Tom wore a broad smile, and Pumpernickel returned to his normal bland personality. The administrator was indeed pompous, self-important, and a tad stupid. He was also kind hearted and truly cared about the occupants at the Hopewell Center.

"Very well then." Pumpernickel smiled after several thoughtful moments. "Larry goes with the group!"

Larry jumped from his seat and hugged Tom so hard that it hurt. Then the jubilant man-boy farted in celebration.

"Oh, brother!" Barb chided.

For the next two weeks, the Hopewell Center felt good, even to Mr. Thomas Tabor, as they waited for their first day at work.

Tom spent each sunny day during that period playing softball with the boys and working puzzles with his tiny group in hopes of building their hand-eye coordination.

The night before they were to start their new jobs, Pumpernickel allowed Julie to give a party for the new group of little people.

The Center provided cake and ice cream. Balloons littered the floor and would cause near hysteria every time Larry would smash his foot down on one of the elusive pastel objects.

Best of all, Tom thought, were the kind and thoughtful gifts Pumpernickel purchased with his own money.

Bernice received an assortment of bows for her thick and quite beautiful, dark hair. Larry actually took his shoes off and put one of five pairs of heavy gray work socks on his feet. Homer smiled like a child at Christmas as he placed the train engineer's cap on his head. Barb's toothless grin covered most of her face as she attempted to pull, push, and tug the new brush and comb through her Don King hairdo.

The room became suddenly still as Mr. Pumpernickel graciously handed Mr. Tabor his gift wrapped in gold paper. Tom was not used to receiving gifts from anyone and felt uneasy as he unwrapped the rectangle package. Tom choked back the almost overwhelming wave of emotion as he held tightly to the leather portfolio engraved with the words, "The Hopewell Center—Where People Want to Work."

Julie then crossed the room and presented Tom with five new legal pads and a box of ten Bic pens. All the little people clapped and cheered.

After the gift ceremony, Julie brought out an ancient record player complete with a huge stack of forty-fives.

Maybe this is what true happiness is all about, Tom thought to himself.

Tom relaxed in the shadows, watching all the precious, beautiful souls enjoy the simplest of moments. Barb's bark broke his point of quiet inner reflection.

"Hey, look over there at old stupid Larry and Homer. Don't they know that boys ain't supposed to dance with each other?"

Tom smiled as he thought of a plan. He wrote his first words on his new legal-pad loaded portfolio.

"Barb, I'll teach you to dance if you will teach Homer and Larry."

Barb read the message carefully before responding. "What the hell?" she grumbled. "But don't step on my feet, turd face."

Unfortunately, the next record played turned out to be a slow one, and Tom wondered what his white shirt would look like after the dance as Barb clung to him like a tick on a dog.

After his slow dance with the wannabe prom queen who still had the new sparkling comb stuck in her hair, Tom motioned for Barb to fulfill her end of the deal.

Tom covered his face to hide the silent laughter as Barb, Larry, and Homer moved in never- before-seen gyrations to the Chubby Checker hit "Come on Baby, Let's Do the Twist."

Bernice sat across the room from Tom, looking sad. *Hadn't she said she wanted to be a dancer?* Tom tried to recall.

He crossed the room, stretched out his hand, and proceeded to the middle of the floor with the beautiful little girl captured in a woman's body. Bernice danced well and stood on her tiptoes to kiss Tom's cheek at the end of the song.

Later in the evening, Tom hoped that the nice, overweight supervisor was not headed in his direction, but it wasn't to be.

Julie almost pulled him out of his shoes as once again to his disdain another slow song began to play.

"Oh, Tom," she whispered. "I didn't realize how strong you were. Hold me tight, big guy!" Julie purred.

As the night grew to a close, Tom returned to the shadows of the room. But this time, Homer and Larry followed. Tom sat in the middle of the boys with his strong arms around both of them as they in turn slept, heads resting on his shoulders.

From across the room, Barb, Bernice, and Julie all looked at Tom with love in their hearts.

What a can of nuts, Tom thought. *And it's my can to protect.*

The Letter: August 18

||||||||||||||||||||||||||||||||||||||||||||||||||||||||||||||||

I just finished reading the New Testament for the fourth time. What a truly amazing book the Bible is. It's like every time I read the words of Jesus, I learn something new. Now I'm stuck on his saying "I came to heal the sinners not the righteous." Oh, Tina, is it possible that Jesus Christ could heal my sins? I want to believe this, but it is so hard. After all, I am the worst of sinners, and what good have I ever done that would warrant any mercy from the Lord?

Although I did not ask for the responsibility, the group of little people seemed to be hopelessly lost without my direction. I almost felt like a big, old sheep dog with a flock of aimless, wandering lambs.

Larry needed my help the most. He would forget the smallest everyday, mundane activity. I swear, I had to re-teach him how to tie his shoes, button his shirt properly, even to comb his hair so that it didn't look like the top of a carrot.

Homer did not need much help with ordinary tasks. However, he did require a lot of love. The poor little guy seemed terrified of any loud sound. Any time a thunderstorm would hit at night, I'd awake to find Homer beside me in bed. There were moments when I must admit I thought of myself as a big, old grizzly bear and Homer and Larry as my cubs.

What can I say to bring true reality to Barb? It is probably impossible to describe her. I do know, however, that Barb was bright. She could read, write, comprehend, and maintained a special wit that caused me to laugh inwardly every time she was near. Barb once told me that she hated every man she'd ever known because they were always tearing at her clothes. What kind of sick human being would abuse some innocent like that?

Now Bernice held a strong hold on my heart. At the age of twenty-three, Bernice thought and acted like a nine year old. But even with her limited mental capabilities, you could sense a woman crying to be let out of a child's mind. She was beautiful inside and out.

Even though Julie worked as a supervisor for the great sum of six dollars and fifty cents an hour, she was certainly borderline between those in charge and the little people category. I really liked Julie, and I felt sorry for her.

At the age of seventeen, she mothered two children, both of whom landed in foster homes. The poor girl did not have a clue where her babies were. I think she loved her job because the little people were now her substitute children.

Julie tried her best to look pretty, but unfortunately that would never happen. She weighed at minimum two hundred pounds, and her thin, mousy brown hair stiff with hairspray and teeth that mostly went east and west would never allow her to be what she needed most, simply attractive. But, Tina, she was lovely. You just had to look a little deeper, that's all.

Even though it was not my decision, the little people needed me. I wanted to run, to escape the presence of new responsibility, *but something deep within told me I could not. After all, Tina, I truly was the only cashew in the Hopewell can of mixed nuts.*

After the "Hi ho, hi ho, it's off to work we go" party, I took Larry and Homer back to the room and tucked them in. Does that sound silly or what? Of course, like most evenings, the boys refused to go to sleep until I wrote them a short story that Homer would read aloud. That night I gave them a real life chronicle. The story centered on a very happy little boy and his faithful dog named Brown. I wrote of their friendship and many adventures in the glorious hills and valleys of Ironton, Ohio. I walked the boys through the special place and could actually see them attempt to visualize and smell the flowers. And then I finished writing describing the most beautiful girl in the entire world, Tina Marie Brown.

After the boys fell asleep, no doubt fantasizing about you, I went back to the solitude of the recreation room. I pulled the plastic folding chair close to the old Magnavox and turned to CNN. Tina, I nearly lost it when I saw you and your husband standing upon the steps before a very large building. You both looked so important. It was then I found out that you were the wife of the governor of Kansas.

My heart jumped like a thoroughbred colt in a meadow of clover. My mind raced as my mouth formed your name. My heart whispered "I love you."

I immediately began to wonder when and how you made it to Kansas. Could this be destiny? Could love so strong have brought us both so close? Then my feeble brain kicked in and reality slammed me to the floor as if hit by a speeding locomotive.

My Tina, my precious Tina, now married to the governor of Kansas and future potential vice-presidential candidate. On the other side of the coin: Thomas Lavon Tabor, mental patient, destitute, unable to speak, murderer, and thief.

My dream burst as quickly as it formed. No, I would not try to contact you. I would save myself from the greatest of humiliation, and I would save you from the ultimate embarrassment. As sad the moment that late evening was, I still found joy in your success and prayed for the first time in many a year that Almighty God would keep you safe and happy.

I lay in bed that night without finding sleep. I attempted to search my mind for the special place, the scent of wildflowers, and the touch of your last kiss. I almost got there, Tina. I could nearly see your sweet, innocent face, and then I heard the screams of Poke and Big Earl coming from the hole I let them die in. My moment of long-lost sunlight turned suddenly black as hell, and I remembered just exactly who I had become, a worthless, hideous, murdering thief.

As the morning sun broke the horizon, I realized I'd hit bottom. There was nothing, absolutely zero left to give anyone. Thomas Tabor no longer existed for any real purpose but dying.

And then, Tina, I felt unbelievable warmth in the room, and I swear I heard a soft, loving voice. Oh, Tina, it sounded like you speaking to me.

The voice gently said, "Take care of the little people."

The First Day of Work

|||||||||||||||||||||||||||||||||||||||||||||||||||||||||||

Julie pulled the van to the west exit door just outside the Hopewell Center dining hall. The sun seemed to pronounce that this would be a special day. She watched the orange-breasted robins hop their way across the freshly cut lawn in search of their first morning meal. Julie smiled as the single white, puffy cloud moved overhead, reminding her of Santa Claus. She took in a large breath of clean air and whispered, "Thank you, God, for my job."

Tom instructed Homer to tuck in his shirttail as he attempted to wash the egg yoke from Larry's face and hands. Barb stomped around in a fury, crunching her face in a thousand wrinkles as she searched high and low for her sparkly comb. "I ain't goin' nowhere till I find my damn comb!"

Tom reached in his back pocket and stretched out his hand with his pocket comb. Barb looked at him and the comb for a long moment before snatching it like it might be dangerous. She pushed her four teeth out in bulldog fashion. "It better not have cooties, turd face."

Tom shook his head in sheer amazement and a bit of disgust as Barb licked her fingers, pushed down on the gigantic cowlick, and pulled Tom's comb through her mangled hair.

Bernice skipped across the room cheerfully singing, "I'm a little teacup ... "

Julie opened the side door, proclaiming, "Okay, my special people, are we ready to go to work today?"

"Hurray! Hurray! It's off to work today!" Bernice exclaimed as she also did a pretty good ballerina impersonation.

"Work sucks," Barb mumbled.

Both Larry and Homer wore huge smiles as they walked out the door to the van, holding tightly to Tom's strong hands.

Julie parked the van at the side of the laundry and walked the group into the plant entrance marked "Employees." They proceeded to the break room, where Julie asked Tom to watch the group until she returned with the owner.

Todd Deaton, the owner of the family business, Deaton Linen and Uniform Supply, entered the break room with Julie and a short, hard-looking man.

"All right, group," Julie spoke cheerfully. "This is Mr. Deaton, the owner, and this is Mr. Austin, the plant manager."

Everyone watched Tom before moving a muscle. Tom rose and bowed his head slightly in recognition of the men. The little people did the exact same thing.

Mr. Deaton purchased the laundry from his father nearly ten years ago. The family was well respected in the small town of Hoisington, Kansas, just ten miles north of Great Bend. After the oil and gas exploration bust, finding employees to do the menial tasks of certain laundry functions had been difficult. Although the little people would not be one hundred percent as productive as the other laundry workers, Mr. Deaton did feel grateful to have the help. Besides, Todd Deaton was indeed a kind man with a big heart. Unfortunately, the same could not be said for the plant manager.

Barb pulled at Tom's sleeve. He lowered his head, turning his face from Barb's stale breath. She whispered in his ear, "That short guy is an asshole." Tom looked at the plant manager sensing the same thing.

"Well, ladies and gentlemen, welcome to my laundry. We are so pleased to have you join the Deaton family."

Tom thought that was a kind thing to say.

"We only have two rules here at Deaton's Laundry." The owner's smile seemed sincere. "Be honest, and treat your fellow workers with respect." Deaton continued, "Several weeks ago we purchased a small towel and apron service that allowed our company to expand considerably. Therefore, we needed to hire additional good people, and that's why we are happy you were available."

"We appreciate the opportunity, Mr. Deaton," Julie responded sincerely as Homer and Bernice nodded their heads in the affirmative. Meanwhile, Barb remained oblivious as she struggled to pull Tom's comb from the undergrowth upon her head.

"Work begins at eight a.m. and ends at four thirty each day. If you have any problems, please feel free to come see me. My door is always open. Welcome aboard, and welcome to our family. Now I leave you in the good hands of my plant manager, Mr. Austin."

"Mr. Turd Face," Barb muttered under her breath, but Tom heard her.

Tic Austin smiled until the door to the break room closed behind the owner. He turned back to the little people, wearing a hard look on his face. "All right, you people, listen up! I know you all ain't what you call normal. We ain't never had no retarded employees here before, so you better not screw up."

Tom thought about how much enjoyment he might get by kicking the living dog crap out of this redneck moron.

"So here's the deal." Tic Austin tried his best to look taller than his squat frame allowed. "Julie here, I've been told, don't have any mental difficulties like the rest of ya. So she'll be the working supervisor for most of ya. All you got to do is fold towels and aprons. Ain't hard, and even a trained monkey can do it."

Tom now knew for sure he'd beat the hell out of this stupid prick down the road.

"All right, which one of ya is Tabor?"

Tom slowly raised his hand.

"You don't talk. Is that right, Tabor?"

Tom shook his head yes.

"That's okay; you don't need to talk to push a broom. You're our new janitor, Tabor, and you better keep this place spotless, or I'll be doing a lot of talkin' for the both of us!"

"Turd face," Barb mumbled.

"All right, then." Tic Austin motioned like he might be leading a preschool group on a zoo tour. "Follow me."

Austin walked the little people out into the plant's folding table area. "Randy here is our floor supervisor. Julie, you and these four work for him. He'll show ya what to do. Remember, monkey see, monkey do. And remember this: if you have any problems, go see Randy. Don't buy that bull from the owner about open-door policy. If I see any ones of ya walk in his office, there'll be hell to pay!"

"Yes, sir, we understand," Julie responded meekly.

"Come over here a sec, Julie." Tic motioned with his fat head.

"Say, none of these retards are going to go nuts, are they?"

"No, sir, this is a very good group. Most are just barely mentally slow."

"Does that mean none of 'em will be writing on the walls or shitting their pants?"

"Yes, sir, I can assure you that will never happen."

Just then, Larry let go with a jumbo fart.

"All right then, Julie,"—Austin tried to sound important—"keep these people in line, and me and you won't have no problems. I ain't never managed no retards before, so I'll be counting on you. Got it?"

"Yes, sir, they'll do good work."

"All right, Tabor, follow me."

Tom walked behind the stupid plant manager, wondering just how far he could put his fist down his throat.

"Hey, Bubba, get your skinny, greasy ass over here!"

Bubba T. Tingle looked like he belonged at the Hopewell Center working in the pillow barn a lot more than any of the little people did. Tall, skinny as a rail, scraggly beard, and a complete set of rotten teeth made him the perfect poster child for hillbilly heaven.

"Yeah, Tic, whats ya need, boy?" He spoke in slow motion.

"This here is Tabor," Tic responded. "He's one of the retards from Great Bend the old man hired."

Tom looked directly into Bubba's dull gray eyes, looking for any sign of intelligence. He found none. On the other hand, Bubba saw danger in Tom's piercing stare.

"Bubba, Tabor here is our new janitor. Show him where all the cleaning crap is."

"All righty the-en," Bubba added a syllable to each word, so it sounded like he said, "All righty, the end." "Whats he a gotta thata pad for a?"

"Hell, I don't know, Bubba—guess its 'cause he's a mute. You know, retard can't talk!"

"Okaya."

"All right then, Bubba; get his ass to work. Start him on the roof, cleaning the lint traps."

Tom contemplated how these two morons managed to escape being institutionalized.

The Letter: August 19

||||||||||||||||||||||||||||||||||||||||||||||||||||||||||||||

Every night when we'd return to the Hopewell Center, I'd force Larry and Homer to shower before dinner. I wish Julie could have done the same with poor old Barb.

After I put the boys to bed and the Center went lights out, I would quietly go to the recreation room and turn the Magnavox to CNN. On several occasions, I saw your husband, Michael. He really talks good, and I'm sure he's a fine man, but I didn't watch TV to see him; I longed to see you again.

During the next six months, everything went fairly well at the laundry. Tic Austin continued to be a total asshole; Bubba, the plant maintenance man, remained a moron; and Charlie Plunkett entered the picture.

Plunkett was the service manager and spent most of his time outside the plant. By the smell of good old Charlie's breath, I say a lot of his time might have been in a bar. The guy wasn't a complete asshole like Tic Austin, but there was something sinister about him. Oh, he was your typical hillbilly redneck in the truest meaning of the word, but I sensed a sick evilness in his presence.

The guy maintained a large beer belly. You've seen, I'm sure, those types that think they're real ladies men. That was Charlie Plunkett. The guy's hairline almost went past his ears. He'd comb his hair over the bald spot, holding it down with several pounds of grease. His pork chop sideburns almost reached down to the first of his multiple chins.

Old Charlie always wore a tie that carried a knot the size of a football and stopped about the third button on his short-sleeved shirt. No doubt he saw something in himself that no woman with any sense could see.

I watched this guy each morning and evening push all the women in the plant into a corner, trying his best to impress them. I sometimes wondered how he talked to the ladies with the ever-present toothpick sticking out of his wide-spaced teeth. Truth be known, I'm pretty sure he took Julie out on several occasions. Can't really blame her, and whomever she chose to date was not any of my business.

Unable to speak, I found, gave me a new blessing. Everyone assumed that because I didn't talk I also did not hear. It was amazing as I quietly went about my janitorial duties some of the things I would pick up. Then one day I heard something that truly chilled my blood. Because of what I heard, I would commit the next sin, an action to this day I'm proud of, and I believe God is too.

The Eighth Sin

IIIIIIIIIIIIIIIIIIIIIIIIIIIIIIIIIIIIIIIIIIIIIIIIIIIIIIIIIIIIIIIIIIIII

At the end of each day, Tom would sweep the loading dock, empty the trashcans, and push all the dirty laundry inside the plant.

The Marlboro-chain-smoking Tic Austin lit a fresh cigarette, flipping the old butt down the dock in a spot Tom had just swept.

"Watch this," he said mockingly to his pal and coworker Charlie Plunkett. "This retard hears about as good as he talks!"

Plunkett pulled his wad of well-chewed Red Man tobacco from his fat jowls and threw it near the cigarette butt. Austin spoke in a normal tone. "Hey, Tabor, you missed some stuff. Sweep that shit up." Both men chuckled, and Tom ignored Tic's demand. "I told you the retard couldn't hear shit, didn't I?"

Plunkett laughed and put a new chaw of Red Man in his large mouth. "Speaking of retards, that little dark-headed one ain't bad! Know what I mean?"

"Yeah, she's kinda cute for a mental slacker, Charlie, but still the same, the girl's a retard."

"Hell, Tic, I ain't asking the girl if she wants to get married. Besides, I've done a bunch of stupid women in my life, so what's the difference?"

"Chances are she won't tell nobody!" Austin laughed so hard that his chain-smoking cough almost caused him to pass out.

"Hey, Tic, let's see what this gal's really got. I'll give her a go, and if she's any good, you get the next shot!"

Tic smiled a wicked smile. "What's to lose—the word of our outstanding service manager, or some grunts from a retard?"

"My point exactly." Charlie slapped Tic on the back. "Here's the plan."

It was all Tom could do not to kill both of them at that moment.

"Hey, Julie, you know your crew has really been doing great lately. I'm going to see the old man about getting you another quarter an hour."

"Thanks, Mr. Austin. I really appreciate your kind words."

"No prob, Julie! Say, I need a favor."

"All you got to do is ask, Mr. Austin."

"Well, I just got a call from one of our big customers, and they're going to need another five hundred towels in the morning. Now, Bernice is our best folder, so let her work a little overtime tonight."

"Gosh, I don't know. You see, I'm supposed to stay—"

Tic interrupted. "Hey, Julie, what the hell's the problem? I've got to stay and supervise till all the work's finished. You can take the rest of the nuts home and come back in a couple of hours."

"Well, if you think it will be all right."

"What's to worry?" Tic said in a confident tone. "Just come back in two hours, and all the towels will be folded."

Bernice appeared to be excited about being selected to work overtime and gave Julie a hug before she left to load the other little people in the Hopewell van.

Most evenings after the owner headed home around three o'clock to work his small farm, Tic, Charlie, and anyone else around would break out the whiskey. Austin took a long, hot pull from the bottle of Jack Daniels.

"So the retard is staying, Charlie. Don't do anything I wouldn't do."

"Hey, where the hell you goin'?"

"Sorry, pal, my kid got kicked out of school for pissing in the hallway. My old lady called a little while ago and wants me to get home and beat his ass."

"Kids," Charlie snorted. "What the hell you gonna do with 'em?"

"Who knows, Charlie? If they wanna act like animals, then I guess you beat 'em like animals!"

"Got that right, Tic!"

"See ya in the morning. Have fun!" Tic left Charlie alone in the plant with Bernice.

The service manager finished the bottle of whiskey, enjoying the warm feeling of power it provided. He walked quietly out to the folding area. Beads of anticipative sweat broke out on his shiny bald head as he approached Bernice, who remained focused on the job at hand.

"Hey, beautiful." He attempted to sound sexy. "You sure do a good job."

"Thanks," Bernice responded cheerfully.

"Say, would you like to have some fun?"

"Um, not right now. Mr. Austin said I've got to fold towels."

"Well, he ain't here now, and I'm the boss!" Bernice, in her childlike innocence, could not perceive the evil before her.

"Okay then." She laughed like the little girl she truly was.

Plunkett held her hand, leading her back to his office.

Pumpernickel did not much care about the fact that Julie left Bernice at the plant alone. "And just where is Tabor, Julie?"

"He had to work overtime too. Gosh, Mr. Pumpernickel, I'm sorry if I did the wrong thing."

"Well, don't worry about it now, Julie. I'll go pick them up in an hour."

Plunkett closed the door to his office and turned the light switch off.

"Oh, it's dark in here." Bernice whimpered. "I don't like the dark!"

Plunkett's breath now hot and labored, he whispered, "Pull your pants down." He kissed the frightened girl hard on the mouth, unzipping his pants at the same time.

"Touch me." He groaned and forced her hand down on his erection.

Bernice screamed in horror, and neither heard the office door open. Plunkett gasped for air as two strong hands encircled his neck and lifted his fat body in the air. With a swift and powerful motion, the pervert's face slammed into the solid oak door with such force that both his nose and erection snapped.

Tom stood over the crying fat man and motioned for Bernice to go outside. He then literally ripped Plunkett's clothes from his body, leaving him completely naked and curled in a protective ball with both hands clutching his broken penis.

Tom smiled as he slowly pulled his thick rawhide belt through the loops. He could not be sure how long he beat this piece of crap that thrashed upon the floor, but when he stopped, every part of Plunkett's naked body carried a thick, bloody welt from the horrific beating administered by Thomas Tabor.

Tom finished by kicking him several times in the face, knocking out several teeth. He then wrote a note and pushed it in Plunkett's swollen, bleeding mouth. It said, "If they act like animals, you got to beat them like animals."

Tom turned and saw Mr. Pumpernickel looking down at the brutalized man. "Are you okay, Mr. Tabor?"

Tom took a deep breath and nodded his head.

"Good!" Pumpernickel stated firmly. "Very good indeed!"

Then Pumpernickel leaned down and whispered in the crying man's ear, "If you return to work here or ever touch little Bernice again, I'll let Mr. Tabor finish this beating. Do you understand me, you piece of garbage?"

Plunkett moaned and nodded.

Bernice stayed at the Center for two weeks before going back to work. Tom returned the next day as if nothing happened.

No one at Deaton's Laundry ever heard from Charlie Plunkett again.

The Letter: August 20

||||||||||||||||||||||||||||||||||||||||||||||||||||||||||||||||||||||||||

You know, Tina, I really get confused when I go back and forth between the Old and New Testaments. I mean, Jesus said to turn the other cheek. But in the old part, God didn't hesitate to severely punish evildoers. I've always known when I've sinned in the past. However, this time I truly believe God was proud of me for beating that worthless pervert within an inch of his life.

After I whipped Plunkett like an animal, Bernice made sure that she always sat next to me to and from work. The poor child felt safe with me. I made a vow at that point to never allow anyone to hurt her or any of my little people.

It was really funny to watch Tic stay clear of the Hopewell workers. Although he for sure hated me, I felt certain the fat big mouth feared Tom Tabor big time.

Several days after Plunkett disappeared, Tic Austin called me to his office. Seated behind his large desk seemed to provide a surge of false courage. Austin swore that if it were the last thing he ever did, the retards and me would be out of a job.

After that conversation, I decided to be more careful. It was critical that I remain there to protect the little people. At that moment I realized I needed to do whatever necessary to take care of the new Tabor family. Because of that thought, I went on to my next sin.

The Ninth Sin

IIIIIIIIIIIIIIIIIIIIIIIIIIIIIIIIIIIIIIIIIIIIIIIIIIIIIIIIIIIIIIII

Tic walked into his buddy's office and believed he saw spots of blood on the brown and tan shag carpet. Even though Austin only ran about three steps ahead of stupid, he sensed something had happened to Charlie.

He attempted to call his friend throughout the day, only to continue getting a busy signal. After work he stopped to purchase a pint of Jack and a six-pack of Bud for the trip to see his friend. Tic wondered why Charlie's red Dodge pickup was not parked in the front yard like always.

After pounding on the door for a long time, Plunkett's wife opened the paint- chipped front door but remained behind the screen. Surrounded by a half dozen dirty kids, and nearly nine months pregnant, Tic knew why old Charlie screwed around. His wife was a real pig.

"Hey, Charlotte, where's old Charlie Boy? Didn't see him at work today."

Charlotte slapped one of the younger children for heaven only knows what and lit a fresh Pall Mall from the cigarette butt she held in her other hand, along with the baby in a stinky diaper. She then threw the butt on the floor, crushing the red glow into the rotting wood with her dirty foot clinging to a yellow flip-flop.

"Charlie's at the dentist," she said as she smacked another child across the face.

"Is he okay?" Tic took a step back, attempting to move away from the stench pouring out of the Plunketts' front door.

"Yeah, he'll survive, I guess. Got his ass kicked last night at some shit-kickin' bar. Serves him right for not coming home to his wife and younguns."

Austin remembered the blood he saw on Charlie's carpet. "When will he be coming back to work, Charlotte?"

"Ain't coming back. Said he hates the laundry business."

"What's he gonna do?"

"Goin' to work for my brother driving a dump truck. Pays cash."

"When will he be home?" Tic knew there must be a hell of a lot more to this story.

"Ain't sure, but Charlie said don't take no calls and he don't want no visitors. Guess you better leave him alone, Tic, cause Charlie seemed real pissed off."

The next morning Tic called Tabor into his office. "You was here night before last, weren't you?"

Tom wrote on his pad and turned it toward his nemesis. "No."

"You weren't here after the van with the retards left?"

He wrote no once again.

"Something happened to my friend Charlie."

"What?" Tom wrote.

"He got the shit beat out of him, that's what!" Tic stood up and leaned over the desk with fists balled, his face so red he looked like a late summer tomato.

Tom wrote, smiled, and placed the pad below Tic's bulging eyes. "Act like an animal, get beat like an animal."

Austin swallowed hard, turning ghostly white. "Get the hell out of here, Tabor!" Saliva spewed from his mouth. "I'm watching you, retard!"

Tom turned to face the enraged plant manager. He slowly raised his hand, the forefinger and thumb made the shape of a pointed pistol.

Austin almost disappeared in his fake leather chair, whispering, "I'm going to get you, asshole," as Tom Tabor walked out the door.

Tic Austin made every effort to give Tom the dirtiest, hardest jobs he could find. Unfortunately for the plant manager, the owner took a special liking to the Deaton laundry janitor.

Six months passed, and all the little people were performing their individual jobs in an exemplary manner. Thanks to Tom, everyone, including Julie, seemed to have grown in ability and confidence.

Late one Friday evening, Mr. Pumpernickel asked Tom to join him and Julie in his office.

"Mr. Tabor!" The administrator sounded unusually cheerful. "Come on in; take a seat."

Tom noticed that Julie also looked pretty excited.

"Mr. Tabor," Pumpernickel continued, "our dear, sweet Julie has brought me a proposition that I find quite interesting."

Julie wiggled in her chair, trying hard to hold in her excitement.

"As I'm sure you know, Mr. Tabor, our center has nearly doubled in the last year—just too many people for the available space and no funds to expand. So Julie has proposed that we enact the Freedom Project for Bernice, Barb, Homer, Larry, and you."

Tom smiled as big as anytime in his life.

"The only problem, however, is how do we find a place that is big enough and, of course, affordable?"

"Can I tell him?" Julie looked like she might explode at any moment.

"Sure you can, Julie."

"Well, you see, Tom, I found this place with three bedrooms and two baths. It needs some paint and fixing up, but we can do that, can't we?"

Tom smiled his approval.

"And now all we have to do is save enough money to buy furniture and a used van. The place is perfect and only two miles from the laundry."

Pumpernickel jumped in at that point. "The place will be available in thirty days. I've called the state agency and asked for a small loan to get you started. If they provide the money and you promise to go and help Julie with the others, well, I guess you'll all be on your own! Is it a deal, Tom?"

Tom almost jumped across the room, shaking Pumpernickel's hand furiously while hugging Julie at the same time.

"Freedom!" Tom wanted to shout.

The next Monday, the state agency rejected the loan.

For the entire week, all the little people seemed to be jointly in a great state of depression. They did not even much care when Pumpernickel arranged for them to visit the circus on Saturday night.

Tom remained in bed that Saturday, informing Julie that he had a bad case of the flu.

After the bus left for the circus, Tom arose and dressed in the navy blue coveralls he had stolen from the laundry on Wednesday. Moving within the hallway shadows, he entered Julie's room and took the keys to her old, beat-up Volkswagen.

Charlie Plunkett's dump truck job did not pay as well as when he'd been the service manager at Deaton's laundry. So now he worked the evening shift at Parkway Liquors.

Plunkett leaned back on the stool, reading Hustler magazine, paying little attention to the man as he entered the store. It was raining cats and dogs outside and would most likely be a slow night, even though the past three hours had been a ball buster.

Charlie raised the paper cup filled with whiskey and water from below the counter as he opened the centerfold picture. He did not see the man pull the crowbar from under his raincoat. Charlie Plunkett also did not feel the blow that knocked him to the floor.

Julie and the Hopewell occupants returned from the circus at just past nine o'clock. She walked Larry and Homer back to their rooms. Tom lay on the top bunk, covered by several blankets. He was snoring.

Charlie Plunkett remained in a coma at City Hospital. The police did not yet have any clues as to the attacker or the robber of Parkway Liquors.

Two weeks later, Pumpernickel opened the large brown envelope received earlier in the mail. There was no return address, just a simple typed note inside that read, "For the Freedom Project." With the note, Pumpernickel counted out four thousand dollars.

Within a month, the little people worked like the dickens painting and cleaning their new home at 277 East Shelby Street. They were now free.

———————————

Charlie Plunkett sat quietly in the green lawn chair, staring off into the sky. Recently, the government approved full disability for the brain-damaged man with the mental capabilities of a nine year old.

The Letter: August 21

||||||||||||||||||||||||||||||||||||||||||||||||||||||||||||||||||||

Well, my precious Tina, we are down to ten days before I go to my final judgment. And now, all of a sudden, I am filled with terror.

It's not the fear of dying; actually, I'm looking forward to the end of my wretched life. I guess my newfound terror comes in the knowledge that I will stand before God and hear the Almighty proclaim me worthless and evil. I pray each night that the Lord will have mercy and just simply send me straight to hell. I can't bear the thought of being before the God of love after all the evil I have perpetrated on mankind.

There is little time left before my execution, so forgive me for rushing through the last part of my miserable life.

I don't know if you will ever read my story once I'm gone and Amos brings it to you. But if it could be made into a book or something, maybe it might help some other lost soul find God before it's too late. If by chance it could be sold as a book, I would ask that any proceeds go to Julie and the little people. Like everything else in my life, in the end, I even let them down.

277 East Shelby Street

IIIIIIIIIIIIIIIIIIIIIIIIIIIIIIIIIIIIIIIIIIIIIIIIIIIIIIIIIIIIIIII

The wood-framed house sat back some twenty feet from the cracked and decaying sidewalk. Most of the homes on the half-mile stretch between Dollar General and Ernie's Liquor Store were abandoned.

The old house needed a great deal of work, both inside and out, but Tom felt a great sense of pride in restoring the place to livable condition for his little people.

The place was small but comfortable with three bedrooms, two baths, a small living room, and a large kitchen.

Larry and Homer roomed together in the bedroom upstairs, which at one time had been the attic. Bernice and Barb shared the room at the back of the house, while Julie maintained the smallest bedroom across the hall. Tom opted to sleep on the couch with the pull-out hide-a-bed.

It took nearly six months to bring the place around to acceptable in Tom's mind. He often wondered how in the world he'd ever accomplished such a feat.

Julie had been a big help, and Barb proved to be a real genius at planting flowers all around the place.

Larry and Homer assisted in painting, which left them most days covered in more paint than the wall was. But in the end, the place looked pretty good, and the little people now lived in their own home.

With all six in the group working at Deaton's laundry, there was ample income to provide a comfortable lifestyle for the little people at 277 East Shelby Street.

Tom established investment accounts for everyone and put 25 percent of their net earnings each week toward those investments. He knew they would need the money when he eventually disappeared.

The first big surprise for the group came just after Thanksgiving, when Julie announced her engagement to Freddy Friedman.

Freddy was a likeable guy with a kind heart and seemed to genuinely care about the little people. Friendly Fred, as he liked to be called, drove a city bus and lived with his mother before meeting Julie at the Dairy Queen one sunny fall day. I guess you could say it was love at first sight.

Tom really liked Friendly Fred and hoped that he would someday marry Julie. He believed that Freddy would move into the little people's home and take care of them as well as Tom had done. Thomas Tabor also felt deep down that his days were numbered. After all, it had been some time since Satan visited. He would not have to wait much longer.

The Letter: August 22

|||||||||||||||||||||||||||||||||||||||||||||||||||||||||

Tina, do you ever wonder why God allows Satan to have a free run on earth? Or why God is strong in the hearts of people like you while the devil totally controls the lives of people like me? Are we predestined for good or evil? I just don't know.

Anyway, back to the story. I guess the last true happy moment in my life came when I celebrated the first Christmas with the little people in our new home.

In fifty years of living, that one day stands out like no other. If for only a moment, I found love, joy, and true happiness. I thank God for that.

Christmas with the Little People

||||||||||||||||||||||||||||||||||||||||||||||||||||||||||||||||

The crisp snow fell like tiny angel feathers all around Tom as he rose early and walked the two-mile stretch to Deaton's Laundry. The early morning air, though cold and biting, provided Thomas Tabor with the sensation of ultimate cleanliness.

He stopped for a moment and watched the thousands of snowflakes fall soundlessly to the frozen earth. *Pure as the driven snow,* he contemplated, something he'd once heard about Jesus.

A small brown bird with a speckled breast lit overhead, his tiny feet clinging to a telephone wire like the world's greatest acrobat. The little creature cocked his head to the side as if he too might be contemplating something much bigger than himself or the solitary man just below his perch.

The diminutive wirewalker chirped away in Tom's direction, as if attempting to tell the man that it was great to be alive. Tom in turn bowed in recognition of his new friend's greeting.

Thomas Tabor remembered a Sunday school lesson so long ago lost. "For his eyes are on the sparrow, so I know he watches me."

Are you there, Jesus? Tom spoke in his thoughts. *Do you hear me, Jesus? Do you love me, Jesus?* Tom knew, like before, there would be no answer.

He pulled the glove from his right hand, reaching into his brown paper lunch bag. Tom retrieved one of the sugar cookies Bernice had made the night before and broke it into tiny pieces on the glistening snow.

The bantam bird swooped from the wire as if he thought himself a mighty eagle and began to dine on the cookie crumbs. Tom smiled at his feathered friend and then headed east toward the laundry.

Today was Christmas Eve, and Tom would only work a half-day. Most mornings, Tom arrived at the laundry a good half hour before the little people.

The old van finally croaked just after Thanksgiving, so the little people were relegated to catching the city bus. That too seemed to have worked out well, as Friendly Fred drove the daily bus route that bought the little people to and from work.

Tom could not really explain why, but he hated to ride on a bus. He surmised it must be the memory of early childhood and the humiliation suffered on the yellow prison he rode to school. In any case, rain or shine, he enjoyed the exercise and considered purchasing a bicycle.

Later that day, Friendly Fred returned to the house with Julie, loaded down with five grocery bags crammed full of Christmas dinner goodies. After unloading the food from the battered pick-up Freddy owned, both Freddy and Tom left to find the best Christmas tree south of Canada.

After a delightful dinner of ham sandwiches, baked beans, and chocolate brownies (the twenty-five-pound turkey would be attacked the next day), Julie called everyone into the living room to light the eight-foot-tall Christmas tree.

Tom fetched a chair from the kitchen so Bernice could climb up and place the angel she bought at Walmart on the top branch.

Larry was then selected to plug in the lights, a task he seemed honored to be given.

"Holy moly," Barb whispered. "Now that's pretty damn pretty!"

"And to us, the baby Jesus is born," Bernice quietly proclaimed in reverence.

Do you love me, Jesus? Tom secretly thought.

"Okay, then!" Julie walked to the middle of the room holding hands with Freddy. "I think it only appropriate that the man who has done so much for all of us pass out our Christmas presents."

"Just like our daddy," Homer responded lovingly.

Tom pulled the kitchen chair next to the gloriously decorated tree and handed the first beautifully wrapped box to Friendly Fred. The excitement and joy in the living room at 277 East Shelby Street could not properly be described.

Freddy sat back on the couch in awe as he pulled the silver Timex from the navy blue box. Julie chewed furiously upon her right thumbnail, praying her boyfriend would like the gift.

"Read the back, Freddy," Julie spoke nervously. "I had it engraved."

Fred cleared his throat. "Love forever and a day. Always, Kitten." Kitten was the nickname he'd given Julie.

"Who da hell is Kitten?" Barb inquired.

Tom smiled and placed a large box before Julie, now known as Kitten.

"Hell," Barb blurted out. "Hurry up, Kitten, I'm going nuts!"

"Maybe it's a dog," Larry muttered.

Julie dug deep down into the wads of newspaper until she located a tiny pink box. Inside she found the quarter-karat diamond engagement ring.

"Will you marry me, Kitten?" Freddy was on his knees now.

"Oh, yes, my darling Lancelot! I will marry you!"

"Now who the hell is Lance-o-what?" Barb asked as the little people surrounded Julie in unadulterated love.

Next, Tom struggled to pull the enormous box from behind the tree. Freddy helped place it before Homer, who looked afraid to open it. Tom nodded his approval, and Homer began to slowly tear away the red and green wrapping paper.

Homer's jaw dropped and he fell back against the wall in utter surprise. After a few moments, he managed to whisper, "I think I can, I think I can."

Two days earlier, Tom had pulled two hundred dollars from his savings to purchase the twenty-car electric train set for Homer.

Julie made Larry cover his eyes with both hands while Freddy went to her bedroom to retrieve Larry's Christmas present.

"Okay, Larry," Julie spoke slowly. "You can open your eyes now."

Tom wished that he could find such innocent joy as Larry reached out, throwing his arms around the five-foot tall teddy bear. It would be the first time the little people heard Larry say, "Yes, yes, yes, yes, yes!"

Barb presented a problem for Tom, Julie, and Freddy. There really wasn't anything they knew of that excited Barb, except candy. But when she opened the tall box and pulled out the red, blue, and yellow candy dispenser with a piggy bank, they instantly knew the decision had been right.

"How in the hell does this thing work, for goodness sakes?" Barb contemplated to herself.

The dispenser held fifteen large bags of M&M's and would dispense an ample handful when you turned a quarter in the opening slot.

"Well, Barb," Julie interjected. "You put a quarter in the slot, turn the knob, and out comes the candy!"

"Hmmm." Barb gave this careful thought. "And what happens to the quarters?"

"They drop to the bank part below, so you can always have money to buy more candy."

Barb smiled so large her eyes shut. "I see," she said and slowly looked toward Tom. "Hey, give me a quarter, turd face!"

Tom had prepared for just this moment and pulled a full roll of quarters from his pocket.

Barb reached out for the quarters and looked Tom straight in the eye. "You're all right ... for a turd."

Bernice disappeared into the bathroom, as Julie requested. Fifteen minutes later she emerged in a beautiful silk and lace ballerina ensemble, complete with ballerina slippers and rhinestone tiara. Bernice fulfilled her dream that Christmas Eve.

"Hey!" Barb shouted. "What about Tom?"

Freddy smiled like the cat that ate the canary and said, "I'll be right back."

The living room exploded with love when Freddy pulled the reconditioned ten-speed bike into the living room. Each of the little people waited patiently to hug the big man who had given them their mental freedom. Thomas Lavon Tabor had never experienced such delight.

Around midnight, Tom stood off alone inside the living room doorway and thanked God for caring about the little people.

Barb's face, hands, and mouth were covered in chocolate as she watched Bernice continue to swirl about the room as if it were opening night on Broadway. Larry lay next to the tree, sound asleep with the gigantic teddy bear firmly in his arms. Homer worked the power switch to the speeding train, periodically bringing it to a halt and proclaiming, "All aboard!"

Julie rested her head in Freddy's lap, fighting sleep. This had been her best Christmas ever.

Eventually the girls crawled off to bed, Freddy went home, and Tom carried both Larry and Homer to bed, sound asleep in his arms.

Tom remained awake all night. He knew there might never be another moment in his life with this much love and joy. He was right.

The Letter: August 23

||||||||||||||||||||||||||||||||||||||||||||||||||||||||||||||||||||||

As we find in Genesis, God created all life in seven days. And now, in seven days, he will take mine. A bit too stoic, huh?

I think I've fought through my terror now. After much thought and reflection, I returned to the logic of reality. I am a sinner. I have done many horrible things. I am worthless and not deserving of anyone's love, especially God's. I am ready to meet my Maker and accept the penalty of my sin. But I go to my judgment thanking God for knowing you and my little people. In itself, that was enough happiness for me.

For the first time in my feeble memory, I have begun to pray. Not for myself, which would be cowardly, but for you, Tina, and Julie, Freddy, Homer, Larry, Bernice, and Barb. Yes, I pray every day that the Lord will protect each of you from the evil presence I have known and eagerly walked beside. If I can believe God will grant that prayer, I can at least go to hell with the knowledge that God does take care of the innocent.

After our beautiful Christmas, life settled down into a normal routine. Our home remained filled with much joy and happiness. Work, on the other hand, continued to be made hellish by Tic Austin.

The man seemed to thrive on intimidating and humiliating others. The little people really did not grasp what the man was doing to them, and I thank God for that. However, I knew what he was all about and struggled each day as he tried his level best to make me feel like a piece of dirt.

I'm not sure, Tina, if things exploded because of a lifetime of humiliation, some of which I admit was self-inflicted, or Tic Austin just couldn't stop until I went over the edge.

In any case, he took me to and beyond the gates of hell. Truth be told, Satan had been waiting a long time for Thomas Tabor to commit the final sin and be lost forever.

The Final Sin

||||||||||||||||||||||||||||||||||||||||||||||||||||||||||||||||||||

The late March wind blew across the flat land of Kansas as if born straight from the womb of the Arctic. The sleet-mixed rain left Tom chilled like never before.

Fighting a strong headwind and struggling against the skin-tearing sleet, Tom decided his best option would be to walk his bike the final mile to work that morning.

He had watched the early morning weather forecast and found it hard to believe their prediction of late afternoon sunshine. He hoped they were right so the ride home would be less tormenting.

Tom parked his bike in the boiler room. Standing close to the four-hundred-horse boiler, he attempted to thaw out. Tic Austin did not see Tom behind the boiler as he plotted with two of his thug employees against the little people.

"Okay, boys, here's the plan," Tic whispered. "Old man Deaton is a fool, and for whatever reason, he loves the retards, especially that asshole janitor, Tabor."

"Well, Tic, he is the best janitor we've ever had, ain't he?"

"Shut your mouth, Gordon. What the hell do you know?"

Gordon was the lead washroom man and always did whatever Tic demanded.

Austin continued. "Now old man Deaton hates a thief more than anything."

"Good thing he ain't never caught us then!" Davey, the stockroom manager, added.

"We ain't thieves, asshole," Tic fired back. "We're just takin' what's due us. Right?"

"Sure, Tic," Gordon responded. "Hey man, we've always been right behind ya."

"All right then, listen up. Today after the routes come in, we'll break into the cashbox, see. I'll plant a couple of the customers' checks in the retards' lunch boxes. My pal Willie is a deputy sheriff, and I'll have him at the retards' house tomorrow for the big bust. Then I'll convince Deaton that the whole bunch of them are stealin' and that Tabor's the ring leader."

"Hey, better yet, Tic, me and Davey will go by their place at lunchtime and hide some other shit, like uniforms and towels and stuff!"

"Good thinkin', Gordon. I believe that dump they live in has a storage shed out back. Put the stuff in there. All right, boys, do we have the plan?"

"I'm with ya all the way, Tic!" Gordon patted his boss on the shoulder.

"Yeah, man. I'm there too." Davey laughed. "Let's unload the retards. I'm sick a workin' around those morons!"

"No shit," Tic snarled. "It's payback time for old Charlie!"

Tom quietly exited the boiler room, walked around the side of the plant, and re-entered by way of the break room door. He waited there until Julie arrived with the little people.

Freddy always had Tuesdays off, so Tom knew he'd most likely be home tomorrow. When Julie arrived, Tom wrote her a note asking that she contact Fred and request he be available early the next morning.

That evening, Tom shared Tic's conspiracy with Julie and Freddy. Together, they devised a counter plan.

Bright and early the next day, Tic Austin went to Mr. Deaton's office.

"Todd, I hate to tell you this, but I think we have a serious theft problem."

"Why, I'm shocked, Tic," the owner said with true sorrow. "I try to be a good employer. I'm fair with all our employees. Who would steal from us?"

"Believe it or not sir, I think the retards are stealing and Tabor is the ringleader."

"My word, Tic. Do you have any proof?"

"Well, last night someone broke into the route cashbox, and I saw Tabor sneakin' around the route room before we closed the plant."

"Is that all?"

"No, sir, not quite. Davey thinks some of the retards have been swiping other stuff. He believes they've probably put merchandise outside the break room in the trashcan by the picnic table. Then Julie comes by late at night and picks it up."

"Gosh, Tic, this is really hard to believe. They're such simple, hard-working people."

"Yeah, I know what you mean, sir, but they are pretty stupid. You know, monkey see, monkey do. I'd be willing to bet it's that Tabor that got the others to do the stealing. He's a hell of a lot smarter than he looks."

"So what is your plan to get to the bottom of this, Tic?"

"Well, I got a buddy—see, he's the deputy sheriff. I thought we go over to the retards' house and look around. Maybe find something."

"Then I suggest you do so immediately and report back to me as soon as you return. There is absolutely nothing I hate more than a thief!"

"I'm on my way, sir!" Tic turned and smiled viciously.

Freddy pulled slowly into the laundry parking lot as Julie kept watch on Davey in the stockroom. Tom stood at the back door after making sure Gordon had his hands full in the washroom. Within seconds, Fred unloaded the towels and uniforms in the back door of Gordon's van. He then quickly drove away.

Tom then moved to the van and placed the route deposit back with the stolen checks inside on top of the other stolen merchandise. He had pulled the checks from Homer and Larry's lunch boxes earlier. Obviously, any stolen cash had been equally divided by Tic and his thugs.

Tic walked into the storage shed, followed by his deputy friend Willie. There was nothing in the shed except a few gardening tools.

"Hey, man, what kind of half-ass wild goose chase is this, anyway? I'm a deputy sheriff, Austin, and I sure as hell got more important stuff to do than this."

Tic was in shock. He felt dumbfounded. Davey and Gordon both told him they'd dumped the merchandise in the shed.

The deputy stood at the back of the shed, laughing. "Hey, Tic, better come here. Looks like somebody left you a love letter!"

Tic shined the flashlight on the piece of yellow legal pad paper thumb-tacked to the wall. He realized it was the same kind of paper Tabor always wrote on. It read: "Hey, shit for brains, who's the retard now?"

"That's it, Tabor," he hissed.

Julie knocked on the door of Mr. Deaton's office. "Come in, Julie," the owner said with a hint of sorrow. "How can I help you?"

"Well, sir, I'm not a tattletale, but you've been so good to us that I feel like there's something you should know."

"Go ahead, Julie. What is it?"

"Mr. Deaton, I saw Davey loading new merchandise in his van early this morning, and, well, sir, it looked like he might be stealing. I don't want to rat on anyone, but I just couldn't live with myself if I thought someone was stealing from you."

"Very interesting," Deaton said, thinking back to the many times he suspected Davey of possibly being a thief.

Tic pulled back into the lot with Deputy Willie and wondered why Davey and Mr. Deaton were standing beside Davey's van.

"Here's your thief, Austin!" Deaton shouted. "Not only is his truck filled up with new goods, but I found a route deposit bag with customer checks still inside!"

Davey looked at Tic in desperation.

"Here are your options, Davey." Mr. Deaton's face was crimson with scorn. "Leave my parking lot this instant, or I'll have the deputy sheriff arrest you!"

"But, Mr. Deaton, I ain't no thief! Tell him, Tic! Tell him!"

Tic just turned away.

"This is a load of crap!" Davey almost cried, climbed into the van, and drove away without a job.

Deaton turned toward Tic. "From now on, buddy boy, you better darn well know who is and who isn't a thief around here, or you'll be unemployed. Do you understand me clearly, Austin?"

"Yes, sir," Tic muttered.

Deaton, in almost uncontrollable anger, left for the day.

Tic raised his head to see Tom leaning against the dock with a huge smile across his face. Austin shook from head to toe with hatred.

Later that day, Tom froze in panic as he heard a loud scream that sounded like Larry. He raced toward the groaning and stopped at the edge of the steps that went to the small, dark basement that had once been used for coal storage.

At the bottom, Larry lay bent and broken. He watched as Larry convulsed in shock, screaming, "No! No! No! No!" over and over.

Tom knew that little Larry was terrified of the dark and also of steps going down. At the same time, Larry seemed fixated with the dark cellar. Often, Tom had found Larry clinging to the wall, peeking down the old concrete steps, whispering to himself, "No, no, no, no, bad place, bad place!"

Tom felt sure his friend did not slip or fall. Someone must have pushed him.

The ambulance pulled away after heavily sedating the distraught member of Tom's little people. He suffered a broken collarbone, along with numerous cuts and bruises. Larry was lucky he had not been killed in the fall.

Tom watched the ambulance race out of the parking lot. He turned, and this time it was Tic Austin leaning against the dock, smiling broadly.

"I guess you retards need to be more careful." Tic's smile was truly sadistic.

Tom fought the evil urges the rest of the day. He wanted to kill Tic Austin. He needed to kill Tic Austin.

It was one thing to suffer the daily humiliation, and Tom could even live with the fact that Austin and his pals had attempted to frame him. But intentionally hurting Larry took the situation to a level that even a jerk like Austin could not envision.

Before leaving work, Julie informed Tom that Freddy would take them to the hospital as soon as they got home.

Julie huddled the little people aboard the city bus, and Tom walked to the back of the plant where he kept his bike.

From across the parking lot he could hear Tic Austin, Gordon, and several of the route drivers laughing up a storm as they drank beer in between two of the delivery vehicles. He quickly realized what gave the group their reason for such boyish celebration. Both tires on his bicycle were flat. It would be the final humiliation that day.

Tom slowly pushed his bike around the corner of the building as he endured their stinging insults.

"Hey, retard, guess you can't call a cab!"

"Tabor! You too stupid to get a driver's license?"

"Hope you get home before dark, moron!"

Once Tom made it around the building and out of sight of his attackers, he gently laid the bike on its side. He crossed the creek that ran parallel to the north side of the parking lot, crossed back over, and stood in between Tic Austin's pickup and Gordon's minivan. Quietly, Tom opened the passenger's side door of the pickup, unlatched the glove box, and removed the same gun he'd seen Tic Austin show all the guys many times. Tom tucked the gun in his pants at the small of his back.

"Hey, Tic," one of the route men said. "Here comes the retard."

Thomas Tabor—laundry janitor, Larry's friend, and major target of moronic abuse—casually approached the group. Their laughter stopped as they saw a truly evil presence standing before them. His smile seemed wicked.

Tic, being the macho leader of the pack, spoke nervously. "Hey, Tabor, how's your little retard buddy doin'? Hope he didn't break his retarded head!"

Nervous laughter broke out and then stopped as Tom smiled, pulled out the .45 automatic, and shot Tic Austin right between the eyes.

The group scattered like young wild quail, screaming like a bunch of frightened teenage girls.

Tom stood over top Tic Austin and emptied the automatic pistol directly into his face.

The Letter: August 25

||||||||||||||||||||||||||||||||||||||||||||||||||||||||||||||||||||||||||||

Five, four, three, two, one. It is now twelve a.m., August 25. In less than one week, I will be executed, stand before God for the final judgment, and be delivered into hell for all eternity. Don't give a man much to look forward to, does it?

Hey, what the heck? I have no one to blame but myself.

I don't sleep much now because I am rushing to finish the writing of my life story. If you choose not to read it, Tina, I will understand. But if you don't, please, please destroy it.

The big guard you met when you visited me has really been a friend in these last days. Sometimes Amos and I sit for long periods and communicate about God and eternity. I'm sure this man will end up in heaven.

Yesterday, Amos brought me a copy of TIME Magazine. You can imagine how surprised I was to see your husband on the front cover. You must be very happy to have a man that so many believe will be the next vice president of the United States.

It is so strange how life turns out, isn't it? You might end up someday as first lady, and I'll be smoldering in hell. No doubt we both deserve our individual fates.

I hope to finish my story in the next day or so. Then I will have confessed to all my sins and be ready to face God for the reward I deserve.

Thanks for caring, Tina. You've been the only one that has. I love you.

The Trial

||||||||||||||||||||||||||||||||||||||||||||||||||||||||||

Thomas Lavon Tabor was immediately charged with first-degree murder. If convicted, he would face the death penalty.

The first week after the murder, the local media people gave the killing minimal coverage. Tic Austin was a nobody, and most people who really knew him were glad, in truth, that someone had popped him.

Several reporters made feeble attempts at researching Tabor's background, only to come up empty. The general consensus concluded Tom to be a worthless drifter that might be mildly retarded. Just another nobody killing another nobody.

The only people in the world who did care were the group of little people at 277 East Shelby Street ... and the governor's wife.

Through wise investments and Michael Klansky's rather handsome inheritance, Tina Marie could be called a wealthy woman.

When the story first broke, Tina went into shock, horror, remorse, and finally the distant memory of innocent love.

The governor's wife worked secretly through her top aide, attempting to secure the best criminal defense attorney in the country. Money would be no object. Maybe she could help Tom through a strong defense team claiming him to be temporarily insane. She had to try to help. After all, she still loved the young boy of years gone rapidly by.

Tina could not believe it when her aide informed her that Thomas Tabor would not accept legal council whether it was free or cost a million dollars. He would represent himself.

The Kansas circuit judge, perplexed and frustrated with the murderer he would pass judgment on, attempted in every way to convince Thomas Tabor that he seriously needed expert defense council. Tom stood his ground.

"All rise!" the county clerk bellowed. "This court is in session. The Honorable Robert Kaercher presiding."

The small courtroom was packed with local news media people, several Austin family members, a few men from Deaton's laundry, and Julie, Freddy, Bernice, Larry, Homer, and Barb. No one recognized the petite woman who wore a scarf over her head and large, darkly tinted sunglasses. She sat to the right in the back row of the courtroom.

To the media people, it appeared obvious that the judge, prosecutor, jury, and the young legal aid attorney sitting beside Mr. Tabor and saying nothing at all detested being part of this regrettable trial.

The prosecutor's case took less than eight hours to present. It was tough to argue against seven eyewitnesses that saw Tabor shoot Tic Austin right between the eyes and then empty six more rounds into his face.

At nine a.m. sharp the day after the prosecution ended their argument, the judge turned to the table where Thomas Tabor sat alone wearing an orange prison jumpsuit. His court-appointed attorney did not speak.

"Mr. Tabor, are you ready to present your defense?"

Tom nodded in the affirmative.

"Please proceed," the judge stated sadly.

Tom rose slowly, walked around the defense table, and stood before the large blackboard facing the judge and jury. He then began to write in bold capital letters. The only sound came from the white piece of chalk as it moved across the green slate, sealing Tom's fate. Without hearing a thing, each sentence Tom wrote screamed out in everyone's mind:

I AM NOT RETARDED, NOR DO I HAVE ANY MENTAL HANDICAP.

I KILLED TIC AUSTIN IN COLD BLOOD.

I AM GUILY OF PREMEDITATED MURDER.

I ASK TO BE EXECUTED IMMEDIATELY.

THERE WILL BE ABSOLUTELY NO APPEALS.

THE TIME HAS COME FOR ME TO STAND BEFORE GOD.

DO YOUR DUTY.

Tom slowly turned and gently looked into the eyes of each individual juror as if forgiving them. One by one, they lowered their heads.

The jury deliberated for thirty minutes.

"Mr. Foreman." Judge Kaercher's voice cracked slightly. "Do you have a verdict?"

"Yes, we, uh, do, Your Honor."

"Please read it to the court."

"We, the jury, find the defendant…" The jury foreman stopped for a moment and looked back to his left. The other jurors held their heads low. "Guilty of murder in the first degree."

Suddenly, everyone turned toward the back of the courtroom as Larry jumped up and began to pound the wall, screaming, "No! No! No! No!"

Barb also jumped on top of the bench shouting, "Assholes! Assholes!" over and over.

With the assistance of three deputy sheriff officers, Julie and Freddy managed to move the little people outside of the courtroom.

Tears streamed down Tom's face as he watched his children from the Hopewell Center disappear through the double oak doors, never to be seen again. He had failed them.

He then stood as the secretive woman in headscarf and sunglasses also slowly arose. She carried a Bible in one hand and waved good-bye with the other before running from the courtroom.

Thomas Tabor was then sentenced to death by lethal injection.

The Letter: August 26

||||||||||||||||||||||||||||||||||||||||||||||||||||||||||||||||||

Tina, I sit quietly sometimes, listening to the other six men here on death row. I am amazed at the fact that each of them attempts to convince the group of their innocence. Is it possible for a man to actually talk himself out of his sin? I can't, nor do I wish to.

God knows what I've done, and his judgment will be final.

The big prison guard, Amos Walker, has brought me a great deal of comfort since I arrived on death row. He's a kind and gentle man who also has endured demons in his past. Fortunately for Amos, he appears to have overcome them.

I will finish my life story tonight and hopefully close out my letter to you—and my life shortly thereafter.

Amos asked if he might make a copy of my story before he delivers it to you. I think I'd like for him to know the truth about Satan's presence and me.

It's funny that my life began with that beautiful little loving child in Ironton, Ohio—the tiny girl who loved me for the person I was inside.

It will now end with the big man in the prison guard uniform walking me into the death chamber to be delivered unto God for judgment. I almost believe that Amos also sees a flicker of goodness in me that you once tried so hard to ignite. Unfortunately, the torrid flames of hell snuffed out that spark of goodness a long time ago.

Amos

||||||||||||||||||||||||||||||||||||||||||||||||||||||||||||||||||||||||

Amos Walker, Jr. came into the world as the first of eleven children born to Amos and Dorthee Walker in Chickasaw, Alabama—dirt-poor Christian folk that taught little Amos the true meaning of hard work and devotion to a God that loved all races of people.

Amos would be the first child within the extended Walker family to finish high school.

At age sixteen, the boy was larger than most men and as solid as a rock. Many colleges from across the country attempted to recruit the all-state defensive lineman, but Amos wanted more than anything to be what his father had once been, a United States Marine.

Amos Walker, Jr. left for boot camp September 19, 1969. His life would be changed forever.

During his two tours of duty in South Vietnam, the hard-working, Bible-believing young man from Chickasaw, Alabama, experienced the worst kind of evil imaginable—people murdering other people without having a clue why.

In late 1973, Amos Walker, Jr. returned to his parents' modest home a hero from the Vietnam War. Yet his Navy Cross, Silver Star, and Purple Heart could not ease the memory of the many slaughters he had readily participated in.

Yes, Amos Walker returned home as a decorated veteran and as a man without a soul.

Amos glanced down at his pocket watch with one eye as he also surveyed the glow from the light in Thomas Tabor's cell.

"Almost midnight," he whispered, realizing at the same time that the man without spoken words was indeed someone he cared about.

Amos stood in the cellblock shadows watching Tom furiously write the final words to his life story.

"Sorry to bother you, Tom, but I was wondering if it would be okay for me to start copying your writings. Ain't no one out in the reception area, and I can run a copy out there if you'd like me to."

Tom looked through the bars at the big man and smiled. He wondered once again if he actually saw a surreal glow surround Amos.

Tom wrote upon a blank sheet from the yellow pad. "Good idea, my friend. I want Tina Marie Klansky to have the original and for you to have the only other copy, if you still want one."

"You can count on I want a copy!" Amos replied cheerfully.

Tom passed the thick hand-written volume through the bars to Amos.

That morning, Amos walked up the metal steps to his one-bedroom apartment above the Laundromat. He did not feel sleepy and decided to fix a large pot of coffee and settle into the life story of his friend and death row inmate Thomas Lavon Tabor.

At 9:30 p.m. that same evening, Amos Walker read the final page from the saddest story he had ever heard. He didn't know how many times in the past twelve hours he'd washed the tears from his face, but his eyes were now bloodshot from the anguished crying and lack of sleep.

Amos closed his eyes, hoping to catch a few moments of rest before he must prepare to return to his post on death row.

The dark, small apartment produced no sound except the hum of the dryers from the Laundromat below. Then the quiet voice came, the whisper that Amos never told anyone about. The still, peaceful voice that often brought him instruction. "Help him see, Amos. Tell him what you've done."

"I can't," Amos whispered in a voice filled with shame and fear.

"Tell him, Amos." The whisper shook his strong, large frame. "Tell him that God is the creator of mercy and love. Tell him, Amos."

The big man listened intently, but the voice did not return.

Amos entered the cellblock on death row and immediately felt a sickening sensation in the pit of his stomach. The ever-present light in Thomas Tabor's cell was not lit. He quickly moved across the tile floor and stood silently before the bars.

Tom was stretched out upon his paper-thin mattress, watching every move the big prison guard made. He noticed the aura around Amos once again.

"Thomas," Amos whispered. "Are you okay?"

Tom immediately turned on the single light bulb, sat up, and smiled at Amos.

"Dang man!" Amos spoke in a loud whisper. "You 'bout scared me to death, Tom Tabor!"

"Why?" Tom quickly wrote across his pad in large letters.

"'Cause I didn't see your light! 'Cause you is always writing! 'Cause I thought you might have gone and done something stupid! 'Cause I care!"

"Thank you for caring, my friend," Tom wrote.

Amos quickly gave the small cell the once-over. Everything appeared to be in order, except something was missing. He looked around the second time, realizing that there were no hand- written papers upon the bed and floor.

"How come you ain't writing tonight, Tom?"

Tom quickly scribbled on his yellow pad. "Like me, the story is finished."

Amos looked down at his highly polished boots, fighting the realization that within ninety-six hours, Thomas Tabor would be no more.

"Tom," Amos spoke softly. "I read your story today, and I've been crying like a baby ever since."

Tom felt like crying now as well.

Amos pulled the white handkerchief from his back pocket, blowing his nose loudly. "I see things sometimes, Tom. And I hear this voice too. It comes to me out of nowhere. I think it is God talkin' to me."

Tom slid down the bunk right up next to the bars on the cell door.

"My brother,"—Amos leaned down close to the bars, separating himself and the soon-to-be executed prisoner—"the voice told me tonight that I should tell you a story that no man anywhere has ever heard."

Tom did not respond, as he saw raw pain, torture, and agony upon the big man's face. Amos quickly walked to the end of the cellblock and returned with a gray metal chair.

Amos Walker, Jr. sat motionless for a long time.

"Tom, I think what you did for your poor baby sister and dying mom was a thing you did from your heart. You was a child then. What could you have known from right and wrong?"

Amos once again produced the hanky, blowing his nose. "Now, I guess what happened to Poke and Big Earl could, in my mind, be justified. And heck, Tom, I'd probably shoot that plant manager myself! And those other things you did weren't nothing most men haven't done. Ain't no one in this world would blame a man for killin' that Mexican, Hector. Man, that was pure self-defense!"

Tom could not discern where Amos might be headed.

"Now, Tom, I ain't saying killing anyone is necessarily right. I mean, only God has the right to end life."

Tom momentarily thought of his own too-soon execution. It would not be God sticking the needle in.

"But you know, brother, God is a loving God, and he'll forgive any sin, no matter how big, if we will only ask him to."

Tom smiled, not really buying into the justification being offered by his friend.

Amos struggled to continue. "The voice that talks to me said I gots to tell you a story that could ruin my life. That you needed to hear what I'd done and how God forgave me."

Tom quickly picked up his pad and wrote, "Are you sure you want to do this, Amos?"

The big man sucked in a huge breath. "No, sir, I ain't sure I want to. But I know I gots to!"

Amos looked to his right and back to the left. He listened to make sure the other convicts were asleep in their cells. He then pulled the chair against the cell, grabbed a bar in each of his bear-claw hands, and lowered his head.

Tom strained to hear the tortured whisperings.

"When I returned from Vietnam, I'd planned to marry Estelle Jackson. She was my high-school sweetheart. But when I got home, Estelle wouldn't see me. Why, she never left the house, and people said she'd gone crazy.

"My heart was broken, Tom. I loved Estelle more than anything. We were going to be married and raise a whole yard full of younguns."

Tears now flowed freely from the big man's eyes. "I later found out that while I was in the Nam, my precious Estelle was brutally raped."

Tom wrote, "Who?"

"Well, nobody wanted to talk, but everybody in Chickasaw knew that Billy Mitchell did it. And in Alabama back then, a white boy raping a black girl was not considered a big deal."

"Was he convicted?" Tom wrote.

"Heck no, man! Got off free as a bird. Said Estelle came to him asking for it."

Tom picked up the writing pad again. "I'm so sorry, Amos."

Amos shuddered as if fighting against completing this tale of anguish.

"Then one day I'd gone fishin' by myself and was driving down Campground Road. Hardly anybody ever drove down there 'cept to fish or to ditch a stripped-down car in Turtle Pond. It was a deep old hole!"

Amos flickered a smile, reminiscing a fleeting happy moment from the past.

"Now just as I turn the bend by Milford's old horse barn, I see this shiny, red pickup truck over in the weeds alongside the road."

Amos shuddered again, wrapping his arms around himself as if suddenly cold.

"And there in the middle of the road, waving his hands like a madman, stood Billy Mitchell in person."

Tom began to sense what was coming next.

"So I pull alongside this fallin-down-drunk white boy, and I ask him if he's got car trouble.

"'Hell yeah, I got trouble, you stupid nigger,' he replies. 'Give me a ride into town,' he tells me.

"I slowly get out of my truck and walk up to him and say, 'Ain't you the boy that raped Estelle Jackson?'

"Tom, he smiled up at me with those big, yellow, tobacco-stained teeth and smirked. 'Hell, boy! I ain't raped no nigger whore—she wanted it!'

"I hit him so hard I nearly broke my fist."

Amos went quiet, and Tom reached out between the bars, grasping his hand as if to say, "I understand."

Amos took in another huge breath, shuddered, and continued.

"When the dirty rapist woke up, I already had the rope I found in his truck bed wrapped tightly round his scrawny neck."

Oh God, Tom thought.

"He cried like a baby, begging for his life. He was so scared he even messed his britches. And then I pulled the rope, liftin' him three feet off the ground. I hung Billy Mitchell in Milford's barn that day."

Tom wished Amos had not made this confession. He was ready to face God for his murders and did not need the burden of Amos's sin.

"I then put old Billy Boy in the front seat of his new red pickup and drove him into Turtle Pond."

Tom's hand was shaking as he wrote, "Does anyone else know?"

"Just me and God," Amos said with painful remorse.

Both men sat quietly for a very long time.

"So I guess, Tom, we are both murderers."

Tom shook his head in acknowledgment.

Amos now raised his hand and looked directly into Tom's eyes. "My mama died fifteen years ago of cancer. On her deathbed, she gave me her worn and tattered Bible. She said, 'Son, what you did was wrong, but the good Lord wants to forgive you. Promise me you will search the Word of God and find his forgiveness and peace.'"

A warmth of spirit had returned to the big man's face.

"I promised my mama I would do what she asked before she died."

Tom quickly wrote, "You think she knew about what you did?"

"Yes, I think she sensed it. But more importantly, God knew."

Amos leaned back in the chair, placing his hands on his knees. "Tom, through the blood of Jesus Christ, who died on the cross for our sins, we can be forgiven and spend eternity with the Lord in glory."

Tom slowly wrote one word, "How?"

Amos smiled and gently spoke. "Just ask him, Thomas. Just ask him."

The Letter: August 29

||||||||||||||||||||||||||||||||||||||||||||||||||||||||||||||||

I finished my life story last night, and my friend Amos has the original in a sealed envelope. If you think it worthy of review, please contact:

Amos Walker, Jr.
21 West Market Street
Wichita, Kansas 86555

Please give him instructions to mail or hand-deliver it.

After review, if you believe there might be any interest in publishing my story, I have executed a letter of consent giving you complete control of all rights and financial gain.

Most likely wishful thinking, but if by chance the life and times of one miserable human being makes any money, please distribute any proceeds accordingly:

Twenty-five percent to Amos Walker, Jr.
Seventy-five percent to Julie, Homer, Larry, Bernice, and Barb.

With just forty-eight hours left in my disappointing life, I now find myself lost for all words. No doubt I should be. After all, my story is just shy of three hundred handwritten, legal-size pages. I guess, I've said all that can be said. My confession is complete.

The warden visited me several hours ago to review all the activity tomorrow before they turn my lights out.

Strangely enough, I had no final wishes except that Amos keeps my Bible. I believe the one he has that his Mama gave him is pretty well worn out, so he can probably use a new one.

I also wrote the warden that I did not wish to see a minister or have a final last meal. Quite honestly, it's hard to think about eating right before you die.

After the warden left, I did think of one wish, knowing full well he could not grant it. I wish I could speak again, just long enough to say good-bye and thank Amos for his kindness. I also wished I could see you for a moment and be able to say the words, "I love you deeply, Tina Marie Brown."

I know you have made numerous attempts to see me during my final days on death row. You will never know how much I wanted to touch you, to hear your voice, to see the smile that brings such joy. But you must understand that although I truly ached to see you, I could not allow that final and total humiliation.

Tina, I'm no good! Why you ever loved me is beyond my understanding. Please know that I will take my final breath thinking of the little girl standing atop the hill before the glorious flowers blooming below in the special place. My last thought will be remembering when you said, "I love you Thomas Tabor." Then I will die.

Thank you, my precious Tina, for being the sweetest moment in my life. I wish things could have been different, and I now wish I was going to heaven, because if I were, I'd get to see the angel that you are.

Even the fires of hell can never extinguish my love for you. Good-bye, my darling, and thank you for loving a wretch like me.

Thomas Lavon Tabor

The Governor and His Wife

|||||||||||||||||||||||||||||||||||||||||||||||||||||||||||||||

Michael Klansky, governor of the great State of Kansas and soon-to-be Democratic vice-presidential candidate, had not slept with his wife in five years. It certainly could not have been because Tina Marie wasn't a beautiful and sexy woman. It was because the good governor tired of women easily, as evidenced by the numerous and frequent affairs almost from the beginning of his marriage to Tina Marie Brown. To put it bluntly, Michael Klansky could not keep his pants zipped.

Tina suspected his philandering early on, but because of her strong Christian beliefs, divorce had never been an option.

"For better or worse," she told herself far too often.

Everyone who worked for the governor knew of his constant sexual exploits. Many men over the course of Tina's marriage attempted to flirt and make advances toward her. But Tina remained faithful, dedicating her time to Christian and charitable activities.

The governor became outraged when he first learned that Tina had attended the trial of a killer. When she visited a convicted murderer on death row, he nearly went ballistic.

For days, he refused to talk to his wife and hired off-duty state troopers to track her every move. He even told Tina that if she ever visited that piece-of-filth convict again he would divorce her.

Tina knew that threat was a load of horse dung. If he were to become vice president of the United States, he better stay married to the woman that everyone admired and respected. She knew it, and so did he.

The night of August 30, the couple sat at the large dining room table. The governor sat at the head of the table, and his bride was some twenty feet away at the other end.

The room maintained an eerie glow, as the only light came from the numerous candles at the center of the table, surrounded by an enormous array of beautiful flowers.

Tina looked across the long table, watching her husband of thirty years butter a crescent roll. She felt no love, no hate, no nothing for the man who would be king.

Tina turned her attention to the flowers, realizing that they most likely were hothouse grown. She drifted back in time, remembering the special place that Thomas had shown her— wildflowers by the thousands, beauty only rarely seen, and a little boy who recognized the glory of God's magnificent work.

The governor broke her blissful train of thought. "Well, tomorrow should be a big day for us."

Tina did not respond.

"I'm meeting with the top people at the DNC and a group of new Democratic congressmen."

Again, no response from his wife, who wished he had not brought her back from the special place.

"And guess who else I'm meeting with?" The governor seemed full of himself.

"Who?" Tina responded with tedium.

"Ted Kennedy!"

"How nice." She spoke with total boredom.

"Well, little girl, how would you like to be married to the vice president of the United States?"

"That would be great, Governor."

He knew deep down that his wife could care less and truly loathed him as a man.

"Michael?"

The governor knew by her tone that she had something serious to say.

"Yes, dear," he said politely.

"You have the right to pardon, don't you?"

"I suppose so." He really did not wish to hear what might be coming next.

"In thirty years of marriage, I have never asked you to do me a favor. Not once have I made a single demand of you."

The governor choked down a large gulp of white wine.

"Where is this going, Tina?" The governor attempted to sound stern.

"For the past twenty years you have lied and cheated on me. Oh, yes, Michael, I know what you've been doing."

"Now wait just a minute here. I—"

"Please, shut up, Michael. It's my turn to talk, and you will listen."

He walked across the room to the liquor cabinet and poured a crystal tumbler to the rim with Johnny Walker.

"Tomorrow, Thomas Lavon Tabor will be executed. I know this man and the tragedy of his life. He does not deserve to die, and you can stop it."

Michael Klansky could be smooth as silk if prepared. Rarely did you catch him by surprise, and when you did, he recovered quickly.

He took a long sip of the warm scotch.

"Let's put this into proper perspective."

"Please do." Tina strained a smile.

"You want me to pardon a convicted killer, one who openly admitted to his cold-blooded murder, because, let's see, because you knew him when he was a little boy?" The governor laughed sarcastically. "You are indeed a lunatic!"

"That might be so, my darling husband, but you are the governor, and you will pardon Thomas Tabor."

"And he'll be burning in hell before I do!"

"Oh, I don't know about that, Mr. Almost Vice President."

Tina walked around the table and casually pulled several photos from her side pocket. She gently spread them out across the table.

"Well, well," she said with biting anger in her voice. "What do we have here?"

The governor's face grew ghostly pale.

"Let's see, Mr. Almost Vice President. Is that you in bed with a congressman's wife? My goodness, what a scandal that would be! You've been a very bad little boy, Mikey. I'd hate to see all your political dreams go up in smoke."

"Bitch," he muttered.

"Count on it, mister, going forward!"

"This is blackmail, Tina. What you are asking me to do is criminal. Do you know the penalty for attempting to blackmail a government official?"

"I frankly don't give a damn, Governor! Either pardon Thomas Tabor immediately, or be exposed as the whoremonger you are. The choice is yours."

Tina poured herself a fresh glass of wine, returned to her chair, and smiled a wicked smile. Then the governor surprised her. He too began to smile and then to laugh.

"You truly are stupid, little girl. Do you really have a clue who you are dealing with?"

"No, why don't you tell me, Governor." She tried to sound brave, but the nervousness in her voice was evident.

"You think some idle threat will cause me to pardon a convicted murderer?"

Confidence returned to her voice. "If you wish to be vice president, it will."

The governor laughed, shaking his head as he reached behind the liquor cabinet and pulled out a miniature microphone.

"So you want to play in the big leagues, do you, sweetheart?" The governor's smile had disappeared. "Well then, let's play!"

Tina moved nervously in her chair.

"I think I failed to tell you, my darling wife, that the dining room, den, and my personal office are all wired for sound."

Now it was Tina's turn to go pale.

"You, my dear, have just been recorded attempting to blackmail the governor of the great State of Kansas. Are you listening to me, darling?"

Tina raised her head to face this political savvy monster as tears trickled down her beautiful face.

"Let's add it all up, then." The governor smiled like he'd just been elected president. "You expose me, my political career is over, and I retire to the islands a very rich man. Now that's not all that bad when you think about it."

"Stop it, Michael." Tina sobbed.

"Not just yet, my darling wife. We must determine what your score will be."

He slowly dropped ice cubes in the crystal glass, which sounded like bombs going off to Tina. He once again filled the glass with scotch and sipped the drink slowly.

"Now, where were we?"

Tina stood and turned her back toward him.

"Ah yes, Tina goes to prison for attempted blackmail, a very serious offense, and spends the next ten years of her life as a convict. I'll truly miss you, darling." He laughed as if this was great fun.

"So what's it going to be, baby girl? Vice presidential wife or criminal?"

"I hate you, Michael," Tina cried softly.

"Yes, dear. I know. But the real question is, do you want to hate me from prison?"

Tina retired to her bedroom, her Bible, and her God. She realized that the only remaining hope for Thomas Lavon Tabor would now have to come from the Almighty.

The Last Night

||||||||||||||||||||||||||||||||||||||||||||||||||||||||||||

Amos moved quietly for such a big man as he walked the dark corridor between the death row inmate cells. He peered into Tom's tiny cell and saw that his friend with one day to live appeared to be sound asleep.

The cell of Thomas Tabor seemed particularly gloomy and dim. The only light came from twenty feet back down the hallway. Amos thought it looked like a cave.

For days now, the big, kind-hearted black man had tried to think of something he could bring his friend—a gift, a token of friendship, just something that might give Tom Tabor a final moment of joy. But then he realized there was nothing of importance one could bring to a dead man.

Without really knowing why, Amos Walker, Jr. slowly slipped to his knees and began to pray.

"Dear heavenly Father, please look down on this poor, humble soul with your loving grace and forgiveness. He's a good man, Lord, livin' in a hard world. He loves you, God— just don't know how to find you. Open his mind and heart Lord; make him see, dear Father. Please, dear God, please take my brother on home to be with you. In Jesus's name, I ask this, Father. Amen and amen."

Amos slowly rose from the hard tile floor, unbuttoned his uniform shirt, and took the silver cross his mother gave him from around his neck. He then latched it around the cell bars enclosing a soon-to-be dead man.

Amos pulled the white hanky from his back pocket and wiped the tears away as he shuffled back to his post.

"It's up to you, God. It is up to you now," Amos whispered.

Tom too wiped the tears from his eyes as he looked out from his dark, concrete grave and watched his dear friend walk away from the cell where he had listened to the prayer of a godly prison guard.

Tom sat motionless for a long period before he slipped the silver cross over his head. He thought, *Are you here, Jesus? Can you hear me, Jesus? Do you love me, Jesus?*

The silence was almost unbearable.

Thomas Lavon Tabor fought sleep with all his might. He did not wish to give up a single moment left before he died. Tom needed to think. But a sudden, deep weariness seemed to grip Tom just after 3:00 a.m. He had never felt so tired in his entire life as he slipped into an almost coma-like state.

His dream began instantly, and Tom found himself back in the special place. Running through the flowers on a glorious spring day, Tom cried out in utter joy as he held tightly to Tina's tiny hand.

"I love you, Tom Tabor," she gleefully exclaimed.

The dream faded into blinding night as Tom found himself standing in pitch-blackness upon the hill where his mother, Baby, and Brown were laid to rest. And then the light appeared. It seemed a million miles away yet brighter than the sun. It began to move slowly toward him.

———————————————

Amos jerked, nearly falling from the chair, immediately realizing that he'd been sleeping, something he had never done on duty before. Then he saw the radiant light glowing from Tom Tabor's cell.

He felt like he should be frightened out of his wits to see such a phenomenon. Instead, Amos sensed a peacefulness like never before. The light seemed to lift him from the chair and gently pull him toward its warming glow.

Tom, now engulfed in glorious illumination, sensed he was awake, but logic told him that he remained in the dream. Then the ghostly figure dressed in the purest white imaginable appeared.

Who are you? Tom thought.

Amos stood directly across from Tom's cell and wept silently with joy as the tiny angel floated through the bars and inside with Tom.

Who are you? Is this my dream? Tom's mind once again screamed inwardly.

"I'm your sister, silly." The angel laughed with childish glee.

Baby? Tom thought.

"Of course, dear brother. Jesus sent me."

Jesus? Why? Tom's lips attempted to produce sound.

"Because, silly, Jesus wants you to know that he loves you and wishes you would talk to him. You better be good, Thomas Tabor, and talk to Jesus."

That very instant, the light and tiny angel disappeared.

The 6:00 a.m. bell sounded, announcing it was time to rise and shine on death row.

Tom awoke to find Amos standing across from his cell and looking like he'd just woken up too. He reached for his pad and wrote in large letters, "Are you okay, Amos?"

It took several moments for Amos to acclimate himself to the surroundings. "Uh, yeah, Tom. I think I'm okay. Geez-o-pete, I musta fell asleep standing up. Can you believe it?"

Tom smiled and shook his head.

"Tom." Amos moved close to the cell. "I had a wonderful dream last night, Tom."

Tom stood up and moved to the bars just inches away from the guard's face.

"I dreamed last night that a shining little angel came right in there with you, Tom. It was as real as me standing here, Tom—I swear it was!"

Tom closed his eyes and thought about the night just past. He wrote slowly on the yellow pad.

"You did see an angel last night, Amos. It was Baby."

The Governor's Mansion

|||||||||||||||||||||||||||||||||||||||||||||||||||||||||||||||||

Governor Klansky felt on top of the world this morning. He'd spent the night with Terry, his new personal secretary, and today would be the biggest day of his life, when he met with the leaders of the DNC.

He peered over the top of *The New York Times* as he casually enjoyed his breakfast of steak and eggs. Tina quietly sat across the table.

"Good morning, darling." He spoke as if he meant the cheerful greeting. "Did you sleep? Well, I hope."

"Very well indeed, Governor." Tina smiled. "I slept like a baby after I talked to God."

"Talked to God, did you?" The governor laughed loudly. "And just what did God have to say, dear wife?"

"He told me that I should go to the prison and be there for Tom when you call with his pardon."

"Funny, dear." He smirked. "I've not talked to God in a while, and as I clearly stated last night, it will be a cold day in hell before I pardon a piece of shit like Tom Tabor."

"Have it your way, Governor." Tina spoke politely. "If Thomas Tabor is executed at twelve o'clock tonight, I will be outside the prison at 12:05 for a live press conference."

"You don't have the guts!"

"Then test me, darling." She smiled and turned to leave.

"I'll ruin you, Tina!" He flung the *Times* across the table.

"You've already done that, Governor."

Amos spent most of his morning beside his bed in prayer. He knew Tom had studied the Bible and believed in God. Why wouldn't he ask for the Lord's mercy and forgiveness? For goodness sakes, hadn't God even sent an angel?

Amos knew he would need God's strength tonight. It would be the worst thing he had ever done, walking Tom down the way to be executed. He didn't have to go, but Amos knew his friend might need his support. And maybe, if he continued to pray, God would intervene and Thomas Tabor would seek forgiveness before it was too late.

The big man nearly jumped out of his ever-loving skin when the harsh ring of his old rotary dial phone exploded.

Amos had no wife, children, relatives, or friends. No one ever called him, nor did he ever call out. So who in the world would be calling?

"Hello, Amos Walker speakin'."

"Mr. Walker, this is Tina Brown. We met about a month ago."

"Yes, ma'am, I clearly recall. I've got a story that Tom wrote and a long letter I'm supposed to give you after tonight."

Tina remained silent for a long moment. "Mr. Walker, I plan to be there tonight, and I hope that my husband will pardon Tom before it's too late."

Amos pulled the phone back from his ear and looked down at it in amazement. "A pardon, ma'am? Please tell me it's possible. I don't want to see Tom die."

"Nothing's impossible, Mr. Walker, if we trust in God."

"I agree, ma'am. I truly do. I've been prayin' nearly night and day."

"Well, don't stop now, Amos. By hook or crook, I'm going to try my best to save Thomas Tabor's life."

"Oh, praise God, praise Almighty God, ma'am." Amos quickly wiped away the tears. "You know, ma'am, Tom Tabor really loves you. Always has, best I can figure."

Tina went quiet for several seconds. "I know, Amos. I know. I love him too."

Dead Man Walking

Tom stood peacefully as Amos opened the door to his cell. Behind the big guard were the warden and two additional men in uniform.

"Sorry, Tom," the warden spoke softly. "I know you don't need to be shackled, but it's prison rules."

Tom looked at the warden, smiled, and shook his head in acknowledgment as if to indicate he blamed no one.

Amos pushed the two other guards aside. If Tom Tabor had to be chained like an animal, he would do it.

Before departing from his cell on death row to the room where he would await his execution, Tom stopped and reached down on the bed where his Bible lay.

"Can't he take his Bible with him, Warden?" Amos almost pleaded.

The warden knew full well that Thomas Tabor was not allowed to take anything with him to the execution prep room.

"Sure he can, Amos." The warden despised having to execute this silent and gentle man.

Tom shuffled slowly down the pale green, tiled floor, taking baby steps in his shower shoes and shackled ankles. The two guards, who had not been seen by Tom before, stood on either side, holding lightly to each of his arms. Amos walked with head down, not worried what anyone might think as the tears rolled silently down his strong face. He rested his big hand on Tom's left shoulder.

Jesse Patterson resided in the last cell of death row, some fifteen paces from the glowing red exit sign that led to hell. His execution was scheduled for two weeks from today.

Tom heard his fellow inmate whisper, "Dead man walking," and realized how profound the statement was. In twelve hours, Thomas Lavon Tabor would stand before God in final everlasting judgment.

Tom thought the execution preparatory room looked like something you might see in a hospital—white walls, floor, and ceiling, with an antiseptic odor most prevalent. The white room of death contained a small, stainless-steel bed, sink, and lidless toilet. A one-way suicide watch mirror covered nearly a third of the wall opposite the metal bed.

Yes, the room was well lit and white as white can be. Yet Tom sensed an eerie coldness within the blanched interior of pale walls and frigid stainless steel.

Tom laughed to himself as he surmised his observation of the waiting death room. It was indeed cold, but he guessed he'd be warming up in hell before the sun rose again.

Tom sat down on the metal bed, not moving as Amos unlocked and removed the shackles.

Amos stood up and placed his strong hands on Tom's shoulders. "I'll be nearby if you need me, brother. I'll be here with you till the end."

Tom rose and looked into the big man's glistening eyes for a long moment. He then put his arms around Amos and gently kissed his cheek. Amos, in turn, wrapped his powerful arms around his friend and whispered, "Jesus loves you, Tom. Please, please, go to him for forgiveness while there's still time. I'll be praying, Tom, until the final second."

"Time to go." The warden spoke remorsefully.

Tom did not look up as the thick metal door painted snowy white locked like a bank vault door might.

"Warden," Amos spoke with a shaken tone. "Can I sit suicide watch until it's time?"

"Of course, Amos. I'm sure Tom wouldn't want anyone but you."

Amos pulled the padded, brown, metal chair to the one-way mirror as he looked through, hoping to witness a miracle, praying to see Tom on his knees in repentance.

The next four hours passed slowly, and Thomas Tabor remained motionless. Then, slowly, he turned and reached for his Bible.

As he had done since Tina delivered the Bible, Tom randomly opened the holy Book, finding Mark, Chapter 2 verse 17:

"On hearing this, Jesus said to them, "It is not the healthy who need a doctor, but the sick. I have not come to call the righteous, but sinners."

Tom softly closed the Word of God, placing the Bible next to his heart. He stood, turned, and fell to his knees beside the cold, steel bed.

Amos, now on his feet, pressed his face to the one-way mirror and raised his arms high in the air. "Praise the name of Jesus," the big man cried out.

Tom remained upon his knees for what seemed like an eternity to Amos. The sinner wept and prayed for forgiveness. He confessed his sins and pleaded with God for mercy and the forgiveness Jesus spoke so eloquently about.

At 7:35, Tom finished his prayer. "You are here, Jesus! You hear me, Jesus! You love me Jesus!" he whispered from his heart.

The large drops of sweat and flowing tears intermingled as they streaked down Amos Walker's face. He watched intently as Tom stretched out upon the bed, clinging to the Word of God resting upon his chest.

Amos returned softly to his chair as his friend fell fast asleep. Thomas Tabor wore a peaceful smile across his face.

The Execution

The prison buzzed like an overcrowded hornet's nest. Word spread quickly both inside the concrete structure as well as outside where the protesters and members of the media waited for the execution. Most of the buzz did not center on the killing of a convicted murderer. The frantic speculation was directed toward the rumor that the governor's wife would be witnessing the execution of Thomas Tabor.

The viewing room could accommodate twenty-plus people. Tonight there were but ten. Tic Austin's wife and parents sat in the front row. Behind them, six members of the local press seemed bored as they mostly passed the final fifteen minutes scribbling upon their reporter's notebooks. Tina Marie Klansky stood at the very back. She did not wear a scarf or sunglasses.

At exactly 11:45, the governor's top aide entered the den at the mansion.

"Sir, I have Brit Hume from Fox News on line two. He said he needed to speak directly to you if at all possible."

"*The* Brit Hume?" the governor asked quizzically.

"I believe so, Governor."

"Well, what ... I mean, did he say why he was calling?"

"No, sir, just asked to speak to Governor Klansky if at all possible."

The governor's frown quickly changed into a broad smile.

"There are no secrets in politics, are there, Henry?"

"Ah, right, I understand now. Brit Hume must have found out that you've accepted to be on the ticket with Ted Kennedy."

"You got it, Henry!"

The governor pressed down the blinking button on the den phone. "Mr. Hume, how nice of you to call. What can I help you with?"

"Sir," the head of the Fox News Network began, "our sources have informed us that your wife is presently at the state prison. We are told that Mrs. Klansky intends to witness the execution of Thomas Tabor and will be holding a press conference shortly thereafter."

The governor's knees almost buckled, and the palm of his right hand stuck to the phone like glue.

Klansky looked quickly to his aide, covering the mouthpiece of the phone with his left hand. "Where's Tina?" he whispered.

Henry shrugged. "Don't know, Governor. She left the mansion around eight o'clock."

"Shit," Klansky muttered.

"Are you there, Governor?"

"Yes, yes," he said quickly. "Yes, Brit, I'm here. I, uh, just had my aide come in with some economic papers."

Hume continued. "So can you shed any light on your wife's presence at the execution and what we might expect her to say afterward?"

"Well now, Brit." The governor's laugh sounded hollow and faked. "Tina is … how should I say it? A bit more liberal than I am."

Brit Hume did not respond.

"You see, Brit, Tina—well, she knew this fellow Tabor when they were children, and well, she's the kind of person that always brings home the stray dogs." Again, nervous laughter.

"I see." Hume thought the governor was lying through his teeth. "And do you know about the news conference following the execution, sir?"

"Of course, of course! She mentioned that she might have to take a stand on the death penalty. I'm sure that's all it is."

The governor continued. "You know how women can be at times, I'm sure, Brit. My Tina has always been her own man."

Weird, the Fox reporter thought.

"Um, listen, Brit. I have Ted Kennedy on the other line. Is there a number where I can call you back?"

"That won't be necessary, sir." Hume spoke dryly. "Thank you for your time." The phone line went silent in the governor's hand.

Klansky began to pull at his hair and in total rage, trashed the contents of his gigantic mahogany desk.

"That no-good, stinking tramp!" he screamed like a madman. "That convict-loving whore is actually out to ruin me!"

Henry moved to the other side of the den, afraid of what the governor turned lunatic might do next.

"Henry!" Klansky shouted. "Get that crazy bitch on the phone—now!"

"Um, yes, sir. Who should I call?"

"I don't give a flying rat's ass who you have to call. Call the prison; call the warden! And if that fails, call that conniving bitch on her cell phone!"

"Yes, sir." Henry left the room, thinking he'd just watched a man go insane.

At 11:55 p.m., Thomas Tabor laid down quietly upon the execution table as the special personnel strapped him down.

The warden and Amos Walker stood just to the right of the soon-to-be-dead man.

"Are you okay, Tom? Have you talked to Jesus?" Amos's voice pleaded.

Tom looked up at the big man, smiled, and nodded, affirming that he had in fact made peace with God.

The big white clock with three-inch numbers slowly ticked away as the second hand moved past the number twelve, indicating that just two minutes remained before the execution would begin.

Tina felt the vibration of her cell phone that remained in her hand, hoping her husband might save Tom Tabor at the last moment.

"Hello," she whispered.

"Have you gone completely mad?" The governor's voice shrilled. "Do you really want to ruin my chances of doing something great for this country?"

"Michael," Tina whispered calmly into the cell phone. "You have exactly ninety seconds to call the warden and save

Tom Tabor's life. Do it now, or be exposed for the miserable person you are. The choice is yours."

"Not gonna happen!" he hissed. "You and your murdering boyfriend can go straight to hell!"

Tina heard the phone line go dead. In sixty seconds, the only person she had ever really loved would be as dead as the dial tone.

Tina looked on in horror, no longer able to hold back the tears. The clock showed one minute past midnight.

Tom lay silently upon the execution gurney, feeling the beginning stage of his death as the calming barbiturate flowed into his bloodstream.

The warden stood beside Amos Walker in the adjoining room. Both men wept silently as they watched the tubes of barbiturates empty and the liquid that would soon stop Thomas Tabor's breathing by paralyzing his diaphragm and causing his lungs to cease functioning begin its drip, drip, drip...

At that instant, Thomas Lavon Tabor raised his head and hoarsely proclaimed, "Jesus loves me!"

Tom Tabor took a deep breath as his head fell back, and he closed his eyes and prepared to meet God.

The warden almost had a heart attack when the red button began to blink, indicating a direct call from the governor.

Before the warden could reach the phone, Amos ran from the room into the execution chamber.

"This is the warden!" The prison's director spat the words out in hate.

"Warden, this is the governor." Klansky's voice reeked with animosity. "Stop the execution."

The warden slowly hung up the phone and whispered, "Too late, Governor—just a little too damn late."

Amos pushed the administering doctor aside and ripped the tubes from Tom's arms. Beads of sweat poured off of Amos as he frantically attempted CPR and pounded upon his friend's chest. The warden placed his hand on the big man's arm.

"It's too late, Amos. I'm sorry, but it looks like Tom is gone."

Then the warden touched the switch that lowered the screen to the viewing room, blocking the frantic effort of Thomas Tabor's friend Amos Walker, Jr.

Amos cried out as if being tortured unmercifully, "Oh God, No! No! Please God, help me give him breath."

The warden could not stand to watch any longer and left cursing the governor of the great State of Kansas.

Tina remained alone in the now dark viewing room, too weary to move, too heart broken to leave.

"I love you, Thomas Tabor," she managed to say through uncontrollable sobbing. "And I always will."

Epilogue

||||||||||||||||||||||||||||||||||||||||||||||||||||||||||||||

The Story

Ten Sins of a Soulless Man raced to the top of The New York Times bestseller list.

Both Touchtone Pictures and MCA Universal were in hot contention for the movie rights.

The life story of Tom Tabor was now worth several million dollars.

The Little People

To date, the little people and their house mom, Julie, have wisely invested $250,000 each.

Their new four-bedroom, three-bath home with finished basement stood just outside of town in a quiet suburban neighborhood. The house was purchased with proceeds from the sale of Tom Tabor's book.

Barb, Bernice, Larry, and Homer respectfully stood in a semi-circle, holding hands as Fred and Julie hammered the beautiful handmade sign into place in the front yard, surrounded by the flower garden that Barb planted the previous day.

The sculptured wood, meticulously handcrafted by Freddy in his new workshop, measured four feet across and three feet high. The design of the sign was that of a big heart. "The Tabor House" was meticulously carved into the wood.

The little people no longer worked at Deaton's Laundry and would never have to work again, thanks to the man without words that loved them so much.

The Governor

Michael Klansky sipped his margarita as the hand-strung hammock rocked gently in the South Pacific breeze. The ex-governor and almost-vice-president of the United States watched the slim and beautiful Peyton Morales exit the deep blue ocean, shaking her long, black hair free of the clinging salt water. They would celebrate Peyton's twenty-eighth birthday tonight with their engagement to be married. Peyton Morales would no longer have to make her living as a high-priced Washington call girl; she would be the wife of a wealthy ex-governor.

Amos Walker, Jr.

The big man wiped the sweat from his brow as he leaned against the hoe and surveyed his garden.

Amos smiled broadly as he pulled a succulent red tomato from the four-foot-tall plant.

He nearly consumed half of the delicious vegetable in one gigantic bite. Wiping the juice and tiny yellow seeds from his chin, Amos Walker looked toward the hill where his two-story white farmhouse rested between ten old oak trees.

"Thank you, Tom Tabor." He spoke as if talking directly into the brilliant autumn sun. "Thank you for giving me a little piece of heaven here on earth."

Amos Walker's cut of the book deal now exceeded a half million dollars.

After thirty years as a prison guard—of which ten were spent on death row—Amos knew without a doubt that it was time to retire. And now, with what Tom Tabor's published story had achieved, Amos could retire in real luxury.

That evening, Amos carefully pressed his navy blue dress pants and white shirt. He would also wear the red tie with a gold cross that Miss Tina had given him. Amos would dress properly Sunday morning when he attended church at the prison's chapel.

The Prison Chapel

The ten-foot-long banner blew gently in the Kansas wind as it hung high above the two oak doors at the entrance to the chapel. "Welcome to God Works Prison Ministries."

The simplistic place of worship was packed this Sunday morning. You could not find an empty seat anywhere, and many of the prisoners stood three deep across the back, dressed in sparkling white prison uniforms. You could sense the Holy Spirit in the air throughout the chapel.

Uriah Mann, founder of God Works Missions all across North America, sat in the front row next to his director of the God Works Missions in California.

Uriah leaned over and whispered to his California director, "This is indeed one of the greatest days in my life. Just think about building prison ministries all across this magnificent land."

"I know, Uriah," Moses Aleeach replied. "And there is no better place to start than here, now, and with a special man that God truly did rescue from the gates of hell."

Tina Marie sat between Moses Aleeach and Amos Walker. She slipped her tiny hand into the big black man's and whispered, "Through God, all things are possible."

"How well I know, sister—how very well I know." Amos fought the urge to jump up and just start praising God.

The room became eerily silent. Not a whisper or a movement could be heard or seen.

From a single door at the rear of the podium, a man appeared, also dressed in prison whites, with a small gold chain and cross around his neck.

He stood at the podium for a long moment with head bowed as if in silent prayer.

Amos couldn't take it any longer, and he jumped to his feet, shouting, "Hallelujah! Praise the holy name of Jesus Christ! I see a miracle! Oh, sweet Jesus, I see a miracle!"

Then Moses rose, raising his hands high above his head and softly spoke. "In the name of Jesus we come; in the holy name of the Lamb we find grace and forgiveness."

When the always quiet and reserved warden ran into the aisle and began to shout, the entire chapel exploded.

The Holy Spirit rocketed through the place, and people cried, shouted, fell to their knees, and danced up and down the aisles.

The man at the podium slowly raised his head, watching the spectacular event that only God could cause to happen. He raised his hands, and the chapel returned to calm.

The man at the podium in the white prison uniform spoke softly. "Thank you for attending the first worship service of the newly established God Works Prison Ministries." The man looked out toward Moses Aleeach with heartfelt love. He then continued.

"I am not a preacher, a prophet, or a holy man. My brothers and sisters, I am a sinner of the worst kind. I have cheated, lied, stole, and saddest of all, I have murdered innocent people."

Tina dabbed at the tears flowing freely down her proud shining face.

"My purpose today is to tell you my story. You need to hear and understand that Satan took my soul at an early age. You need to know that there is hope, forgiveness, and grace. You must come to realize that only God can provide the most unbelievable peace necessary to heal the wounds of a sinner like me. Today is your opportunity to reach out and touch Jesus."

For the next thirty minutes, the man at the podium told his life story. There was not a dry eye in the place as he concluded.

"I know for many of you, it is difficult to believe. Does Jesus see you? Yes he does! Does Jesus hear you? If you call out to him! Does Jesus love you? Like no one else ever could.

"How do I know these things, you might ask? I know these things because God forgave a wretch like me. I know because I have the peace and love of Jesus Christ in my heart."

The man paused for several seconds. "I know,"—his voice was near a whisper—"I know because I, Thomas Lavon Tabor, returned from hell by the saving grace of Jesus Christ."

He reached his arms toward the audience. "Come now." His voice seemed almost angelic. "Come find peace and joy in the love of Jesus."

Seventy-seven inmates found God that Sunday morning in the prison chapel.

Washington, D.C.

One year after Tom Tabor helped begin God Works Prison Ministry, Uriah Mann and Moses Aleeach waited nervously in the room outside the Oval Office.

Uriah carried a portfolio of letters from both senators and the new governor of Kansas. He also had pardon recommendations from the warden, the director of federal prisons, and most of the religious leaders across the country.

Unfortunately, the president of the United States believed that all criminals should do their time to the very last day.

The Visitor's Room

"I went to see Julie and the little people yesterday."

Tom smiled. "So how is my adopted family doing?"

"They are doing great, Thomas," Tina replied. "And Julie said they would be praying for you throughout today."

"How sweet, Tina, the prayers of the innocent."

Just then, the outer door to the visiting room opened. The warden walked in, followed by Amos Walker, Jr. The expression of both men's faces appeared sullen.

Amos walked slowly over to Tom's table and rested his bear paw upon his friend's left shoulder. He seemed afraid to speak. Then a tiny smile began to spread across Amos's broad face.

"Will chicken and dumplings be all right for dinner tonight?"

"Huh?" Tom inquired, totally confused.

"You've been pardoned." The warden beamed. "Go pack your things, Tom. You are a free man."

Tina threw her arms around Tom as both wept joyfully. Amos too let the tears flow as he witnessed the love between a godly woman and the man he had brought back to life on the execution table.

Tom pulled back, slightly caressing the tiny, smooth hand of the woman he loved. He kissed the simple gold ring on her finger.

Tina placed both hands on the free man's strong face. "I love you, Thomas Lavon Tabor—always have and always will."

Tom looked deep into her crystal blue eyes and for an instant thought he saw the wildflowers in full bloom at the special place.

Brushing back her golden hair, Thomas Lavon Tabor responded, "I love you too, Tina Marie Tabor."

e|LIVE

listen|imagine|view|experience

AUDIO BOOK DOWNLOAD INCLUDED WITH THIS BOOK!

In your hands you hold a complete digital entertainment package. In addition to the paper version, you receive a free download of the audio version of this book. Simply use the code listed below when visiting our website. Once downloaded to your computer, you can listen to the book through your computer's speakers, burn it to an audio CD or save the file to your portable music device (such as Apple's popular iPod) and listen on the go!

How to get your free audio book digital download:

1. Visit www.tatepublishing.com and click on the e|LIVE logo on the home page.
2. Enter the following coupon code:
   b868-833b-729b-8c26-ca94-77d7-036f-608e
3. Download the audio book from your e|LIVE digital locker and begin enjoying your new digital entertainment package today!